THE
CREST HILL
MU7DERS

THE
CREST HILL
MU7DERS

ISSAC BROOKS

CONTENTS

PROLOGUE

I have been through a lot. Love is not a thing I take likely. I mean, for a long time now, I doubted it was even a real thing. Sure, I see many people on TV say they are in love, but that's all just acting. Love is something you feel, and it can make you do silly things. Like skulking in the dark. I could not help but smile to myself as I silently watched her lock the door to the diner. It was almost like she wanted us to be alone, though to be honest, she had no idea that I was even there. I did not mind though; it made the whole thing feel like we were playing a game of hide and seek. This was different though… I was hiding just as much as I was seeking.

Soon I will be the only thing on her mind. But first, I have to remain in the shadows. It's far too early for me to get ahead of myself. I do not want to ruin this one. The time will come for her to know me and all the lovely ideas I have planned for us, and then she will know how much love I truly have for her. I bet she's already unto me; she's super smart, so it wouldn't surprise me if she was. She must know I love her- I'm not as mysterious as I think I am. In a way, we have already met. How weird would it have been if I had approached her out of the blue when she had no idea who I was- that would only scare her away. She knows me, but I know her more. I mean, the relationship only works if one partner is more invested than the other.

I remember it vividly; it was a cold night, and she was dressed in long pants and a thick jacket. I noticed she was wearing a plaid shirt underneath the jacket when she served me while I was sitting at the counter. And as usual, she smiled fondly at me when she poured me a mug of coffee. She works here and smiles a lot like everyone else working the counter when on duty. I get that she has to smile at the customers but mine was different. I am not naïve; I know what love looks like. When she smiles at me, it's different from when she has her obligatory show of teeth with the others, it's unique and if that was not an indication that she loves me, I do not know what is. She had a lovely smile; honestly, I wish I was the only one who got to see it.

She has to be the most beautiful woman I have ever seen. I do not know where to begin with the details; everything about her is alluring. Her long black hair had blonde streaks in it, a touch I liked very much- it made her stand out. It gave away her need for attention.

Her eyes are like large and brown gems. I could be lost in them for hours… they made it easy so I could see everything she was feeling. A perfect doorway to her soul. That was how I knew that she had fallen in love with me. Her eyes betrayed her heart. Her eyes always have this way of lighting up whenever I walk into the diner.

'Oh, did I forget to mention that she is beautiful? She was charming and petite too- she could fit perfectly into my arms, and I like that the most about her.'

I always follow her from work. There are a lot of sickos out there but so long as I'm around, she will always be safe. That's why I follow her… to keep her safe, nothing more. I'm content with playing her guardian angel. I know her route, and I am glad she is into routines just as I am. That proved it, we are practically soul mates- she was made for me. I made my steps match hers from the other side of the road while we walked. I did not want her to hear me skulking in the shadows. It would have defeated the purpose of making her feel secure if she saw me. I never want her to feel like I'm overprotective or overbearing. She always has a spring in her steps. She is this kind of energetic go-getter that hardly ever looked stopped to look behind her, which made her oblivious to me most of the time, it was not a good trait of hers but it's because she's like this that it's easy for me to shield her. I wouldn't be wrong to say she's so carefree because she knows she's got me looking out for her.

Her house is a few blocks away from the diner, I had the address memorized just in case I'd ever need it. We have walked the same path every day for the past three weeks. It's a straight route with no corners or turns, and I'm comfortable with that. I would have been afraid for her safety if it had any alleys. So, you can imagine my surprise when something odd happened.

Today is different; she's taking a detour. I'm not worried; why would I be? She's human after all. I'm a little surprised though. She never takes a detour, it's either she's heading home, to the diner, library, or somewhere close by. Today she was going somewhere new. This is shocking. Our relationship is hinged on the fact that we are both creatures of habit… but it's fine. I won't let this rattle me; it's fun to change things now and then, so let's see where you are going.

I followed her, careful not to draw any unwarranted attention to myself. Then I heard his deep, raspy voice in my ears- ***"I told you. She is just like Sophia."*** I paused and took a deep breath when I shook my head, trying so desperately to dispel the voice. 'No. She's different. She really loves me, just as much as I love her.' I thought but in the end, my thoughts were nothing more than whispers to his voice.

"Shut up! She is not!" I whispered to the voice. Instead of shutting up, it broke out in a burst of uncontrollable laughter that annoyed me. It was always like this, taunting me. The voice was always trying to get me to second guess myself. At times it's so annoying that I would have clawed it out of my head ages ago if I could. Sometimes I would beat myself up over it but today was different. I was not going to let this voice distract me. I ignored it with a straight face as I followed her, I have come to terms with reality. There is no way to rid myself of the voice truly. All I can do is tone him out by counting, so I did. As I did, I heard his haunting laughter diminish into a whisper and then it was gone.

I heaved a sigh of relief and walked on. I had lost her and as infuriating as it was, I managed to keep my composure. I don't know where she is, but I know exactly where she will be. After all, what kind of man would he be if he did not keep his woman safe.

I stood outside her apartment and waited patiently. Patience was a virtue, one that I had plenty of.

And my patience was rewarded. Not long after, she returned to the comfort of her apartment, but she was not alone. She had another man with her, the bastard was a tall, muscular man and his dirty hands were holding her around the shoulders.

The voice I had fought to down burst into deep scornful laughter, screaming **"I told you."** over and over again. I slammed my fist into a tree and gritted my teeth.

I stood in the shade across the road from her house along Sandhill Street and watched as this 'new man' hugged her tightly before letting her walk into her house and shut the door. As he left, he had this cocky grin on his face, and he must have felt like the luckiest man alive. I can't shake this knowing feeling that I've seen his ugly face somewhere else before now.

"Like what you see?" Its voice smirked as I turned my back to the house and sulked. It would not shut up, nagging me as I walked away from her house. My chest hurt so badly that I had to hold my hand over it to steady myself. My heart felt like it had burst; I was heartbroken. When I refused to answer, the voice returned to taunting me, laughing viciously as I banged my hand against my head seven times to shut him up.

"No…" I whispered to myself, "He just walked her to her house. She did nothing wrong." My lover is flawless, if anything, I need to do better at taking care of her.

She's sweet; sweet things always attract ants. That's what he is… an ant, a pest! **"You saw it, didn't you?"** For once, the voice has a point; it makes perfect sense now. That man… He's evil. I saw it, the mark. He had a mark on his forehead. I will have to protect my woman from this evil. I have to.

CHAPTER
ONE

A cool breeze blew through her hair as she strolled nervously through the neighborhood. The streetlights gave the night streets beneath them a charming hue that she took a moment to admire on her way. It was so quiet and tranquil that it gave her an unnerving sense of dread when she allowed her thoughts to wander further than the path before her. Sophia had to admit it to herself, 'This would have been a good day for a walk if the neighborhood was a little safer.'

Just the other night, one of the neighbors insisted they had noticed a shady figure stalking them. Sophia did not take the story likely. It might have just been a trick of the night planning on their sight, it would not have come as a surprise to her, but now Sophia was convinced she was being followed. She was easily prone to paranoia, the kind of paranoia that had always looked over her shoulder. She usually walked at a gracefully moderate pace, but with every glance behind her, she was uneasily increasing her strides. She was a startle away from darting down the street in a sprint.

She could not shake the uneasy conviction that she was being followed. Sophia was starting to second guess herself; taking a walk so late at night no longer became a logical decision as it was when she literally ran out on her mother. Now wondered why she had decided to get out so late in the day in the first place. No one could blame her for being so restless. Staying at home had been making her feel suffocated for quite some time now.

Riley, Sophia's mother had not been herself lately. She had begun to burn incense ever so often and Sophia could not stand the smell. Riley said it had a charming effect on it. Actually, it had the opposite effect on her daughter. If Sophia got her way even for a second, she was very sure she would toss them all out at the drop of a hat.

The apartment her mother rented on Weeping Willow Street was cozy but so small the smell of her burning incense would permeate through the walls and find its way into every room in the apartment in mere minutes. Her mother had always been a religious zealot, even more so now her husband, Philip, had left them for a younger woman. Sophia did not have a problem with that. However, the only problem was that Sophia's mother had trouble keeping to a single faith. One minute she worshiped a Buddha, the next, it was some deity she had never heard of. In fact, Sophia was convinced her mother was confused because her gods seemed to change with every passing week.

To be honest, the nauseating stench of incense was the least of Sophia's troubles. She simply wanted to get away from it all. The place brought back memories, fond memories. It reminded her of when everything was perfect, and they were actually a happy family-not the fragmented mess they are now. It was sweet at times, but in the end, the memories made left her feeling bittersweet about the present.

Earlier that day, Riley was having one of her 'episodes. When the incense and the meditating did not seem to do the trick, her mother would go into rage ranting and raising a fuss about everything wrong with the world. Today, her mother had started crying and cursing at Sophia's father, blaming him for wrecking her.

Sophia knew she had to get out of the house. All the negative energy had slowly begun to seep through the cracks in Sophia's demeanor, and everything began to feel like they were closing in on her. Sophia felt a slight relief. She was at least glad that she no longer lived with her mother. Sophia had escaped to her mother's home for a short time, feeling she needed a little time to piece her own life together.

She did not want to trouble her mother with any of her own troubles; she did not want to think about it either. Sophia imagined how silly she must have looked, leaving her mother's place the way she did. She left in so hurry that it gave anyone who saw her the impression she was fleeing for her dear life (Luckily, no one saw her leave). Her mother lived on the third floor and with no elevator, Sophia all but ran down the three flights of stairs out of the building. She was in such a hurry that she bumped into a lady walking in as she stepped out the main entrance.

"Sorry." She said without looking up, walking away quickly. Sophia could not tell if her apology was any use because she heard the lady murmur after her. She felt bad, but her urge to get away from her mother's place overcame her manners, so she pressed on ignorantly. She wanted to return to her place before it got too dark. The streets were the same as they had been when she had left Crest Hill almost ten years ago. If she let her mind wander, she realized that almost every corner on the street brought back memories. It was just like her mother's place. Many of them were bittersweet.

Sophia did not like how easy it was for nostalgia to turn melancholic when it came to her. 'Ten years!' as she slowed her pace approaching the Crest Hill gate. It seemed like a lifetime ago and in many ways, it was. Those were simpler times when the most pressing issues revolved about her deciding what to wear to school, who had a crush on who, and cheer practice. Those were simpler times. Now life had taken on a more complicated tone. Sophia longed for those simpler times. She sighed and shrugged, trying to keep the sudden tears at bay.

She took a detour into school and walked around the school for a bit. Shocking how adventurous she had gotten despite being scared enough to jump at shadows just a moment ago. Sophia was actually surprised she had made it in without bumping into any security. She recognized most of the classrooms, but her curiosity peaked as she went towards the newer rec center the school had added. The entire school was eerily still, that was no surprise. The place was entirely empty after all, and yet Sophia was not unnerved by the loneliness; rather, she felt unnaturally calm exploring its premises.

Sophia graduated from Crest Hill High School almost ten years ago; being on school grounds brought back more memories than strolling by ever. It felt just like yesterday. She was cheerleading with her squad as the football team practiced and stole glances, checking them all out.

Riley and Paul… her parents, had still been together back then. In all her days, never had she imagined that her life would have taken a turn for the worse after high school. Sophia was not the pompous type, but back in high school, she was undoubtedly top of the world. Now, none of that, she was just another pretty face. Other than that, she had nothing really going for her.

Sophia did not have a lot of friends these days. All her old friends had moved away from Crest Hill after graduating and it was only a matter of time before many of them felt out of touch. Sophia had thought going to college would change everything, and everything did change- just not the way she thought they would.

She sighed, thinking about it now; she did not have a say in the way things went. She did not want to think about it; everything seemed to only grow depressingly with the years that followed. She had a smile on as she continued through the school property. There was a grove of trees just beside the gym, where she and her friends had met up back in the day to hold wild parties. She stood inside the grove, allowing herself to reminisce for a moment.

It was a fond memory, so fond she wondered why it made her tear up. She missed them. Sophia remembered the last party they held there. It was the night before graduation. It was also the day she had found out Ken, her boyfriend, had been cheating on her all through their senior year and with her so-called best friend, Brooke, at that.

To make things worse, her father had come to her graduation with Dalia- Sophia did not know she was his girlfriend at the time. Riley on the other hand… quickly saw through her husband's bullshit. Her mother was so furious she caused a scene ruining everything. Now that she thought about it, Sophia guessed that was probably a detail all her friends were bound to remember. The crazy woman's daughter.

After that, Sophia could not have gotten out of Crest Hill any soon. She thought leaving was the best thing for her. Now she was back on a trip down memory lane, it was almost like time had not passed. It stood still and waited for her. Sophia sighed and sniffed, allowing the tears she had tried to hold back to drip down her cheeks.

She could have sworn she heard something and was startled as she whirled around trying to spot whatever must have startled her. It was much too dark for her to tell where it had come from, but it was safe for her to conclude she was alone. Solitude did not comfort her. Sophia remembered something. There was this story she heard back in the day, no one in Crest Hill could say they had not heard the story of the woman in the woods. It was about a woman found dead in the woods close to the school after a summer break.

One of the students claimed to have seen her. The woman was so pretty and dolled up that she was a sight to behold even in death. Whoever offed her went out of their way to make her look good before carving the number 7 unto her forehead. Sophia shivered at the thought; now she wished it was just a rumor but remembering how the whole school had buzzed with the story- it had to be true.

Either it was, or someone got in trouble for being a bloody good storyteller. Sophia would rather believe it was all made up than entertain the possibility of a killer being on the loose. As time went by, students had come up with different variations of the story, each more bizarre and fantastical than the last, but none of them seemed to have an ending where the killer was ever apprehended. 'Stop it…' Sophia sighed and shook her head to dispel the eerie thoughts running around her head. It was a bad habit of hers, over-thinking.

"Where did the time go?" Sophia muttered to herself, using the back of her hand to wipe her cheeks. It got darker than she wanted it to get, time flew by her during her little sidetrack and now it was awfully late. She had gotten enough of her detour and hurried back out of the school's premises, thinking about that dumb story that had ruffled her feathers. Now being on the street alone felt creepier than it did the first time. She never noticed how long the walk from school was, most likely because she always had her pals by her side in all her memories of walking from school.

It was a cool night. She drew her small jacket closer to her body, suddenly feeling chilly. The gentle night breeze had started to blow her way, but Sophia knew better; she was more afraid than cold. Though it was a bit chilly that night, this was the middle of summer, and the weather was generally warm. She only felt chilly because she was feeling a bit uneasy, and it was all in her head.

The night was already dark and eerie enough to dishearten the boldest of men and then she heard a loud crash like something had fallen over in the distance behind her. It might have been distant, but the disturbance was nearly enough to startle her soul out of her body. Sophia spun with her eyes wide in suspicion to discover that there was nobody there, the street behind her was dark and lonely. A raccoon had simply raided a trash can and knocked it over. She took a deep breath and muttered to herself; she was annoyed she had let her mind play tricks on her.

Sophia hated that she was such a scaredy-cat. She waited for a moment just to be sure that nothing was lurking in the shadows behind her and of course, there was nothing there; even if there were, she was clowning herself to believe she could have seen them. She then quickly whipped forward and bumped right into somebody. She stumbled backward and fell on her butt with a scream in her lungs. Sophia broke into a cold sweat but had managed to hold herself from screaming, instead she cursed loudly.

She looked up and then sighed in relief; she recognized the person in front of her. It had been quite some time, but she recognized him. "My bad should have watched where I was going…" She apologized with an embarrassed laugh to herself as he decided to be a gentleman and helped her up, "But damn it- you scared me."

Sophia was glad that he did not seem annoyed by her, unlike the lady she had run into earlier that evening. As she looked at him, she noticed the years seemed to have been easy on him.

"I'm so sorry, I didn't mean to." He laughed wryly.

Sophia smiled like an idiot, she felt like one too for having forgotten his name. He had one of those faces that left a lasting impression but in the end, she was still bad with names. She quickly averted her eyes when he looked at her with a broad smile. She was embarrassed but that was not all. 'Oh no.' she thought dreadfully. He had this playful aura about him. It was no argument that he was excited to have run into a familiar face; sadly, the feeling was not mutual. They might have gone to the same high school, but Sophia was never fond of him; she always considered him to be weird.

"Hey, Sophia. It's been a while, how lucky am I? You still live around these parts?" He said with a broad smile on his face. Even though he looked better physically, Sophia sensed that he was still the same person underneath it all. He was always so bubbly and friendly but then he came off as eager and naive.

'Lucky…' Who considers themselves lucky for such an odd encounter. Sophia smiled and shrugged; she was at least glad it was a familiar face she had run into, but she was in no mood for reunions. "Yeah. I have been out of town and just returned home for a few days." Sophia explained.

He nodded, staring intently at her. "I could walk you if you like?"

'Weren't he going somewhere?' She thought behind her awkward grin.

She remembered that he was this way in high school, always paying her unwanted attention. It was sweet at first, but it got annoying and overbearing somewhere down the line. Almost like he was smothering her with his goodness. He was not a bad guy but for some reason, Sophia just had a hard time dealing with his kind. Right now, she only wanted to be left alone so she could crawl under her sheets and scold herself for being so jumpy.

"Nah… I'm good," She replied, trying to be polite and take his attention away from herself, she was hopeful his name would come to her before they were done talking. Then they could both on their separate ways. "So, what about you? How have you been?"

He just shrugged and said, "So-so."

He kept staring at her; his eyes lit up like fireworks. It was like she was staring back at a love-struck puppy, making her uncomfortable.

Sophia quickly turned away. She did not know what to say to him. He stirred up memories she would have rather left forgotten. He once had a crush on her, but that did not end well. She had no choice. He was just as awkward then as he was now, and she had to tell him off for being annoying.

But then, what was she thinking? Of course, he would be over it, and it had been ten years ago. 'He couldn't still be mad at me, I mean… we were just dumb kids. Sure, as hell! doesn't have a crush on me anymore… right?'

'Way to go, Sophia. You're still the same conceited girl you were in high school,' she berated herself on the way; though she had tried to turn him down, he still decided to walk her.

Sophia sighed; they had reached her apartment building, saving her from the awkward silence that had plagued them. Only God knows what he had heard about her while she was off at college. This was a small town; everybody knew everybody's business.

"Well, this is me." She said, gesturing to the building. "It was nice seeing you again."

He only nodded and smiled at her. She quickly walked into the apartment but before she took the stairs, she turned back to find him still staring after her. She waved at him, and he waved back as she took the stairs two at a time. The Sooner she was in her room, the better she would feel.

THERE'S THIS THING ABOUT MEMORIES THAT MAKE YOU feel complete, but then again, your memories could just as easily break you. Earl, for instance, remembered that day in high school clearly. Almost like he was haunted by it. That morning, he had left Johnson's ranch quite early and had dressed in his best shirt and slacks. In his sixteen-year-old mind, he had found the love of his life in Sophia and was going to make her his.

His foster father, Mr. Johnson was a nice enough man and mostly allowed them to do whatever they wanted, especially since he had lost his wife. He and his wife had taken good care of him and the other foster kids. It was a pity his wife had died, and he had lost motivation for anything. That was why he had stopped homeschooling them and sent them to regular school instead. Neil and Molly were both in High school. They were the remaining foster kids assigned to Mr. and Mrs. Johnson at the time. They had been with them long before Earl had joined the lot.

Everything had to go as planned, and Earl remembered thinking. He was going to confess his love to Sophia, and nothing was going to stop him. Earl had fallen in love with Sophia, not only because he considered her the most beautiful girl in the whole school but also because she had been the only person who had befriended him since he started at their school. He had joined the class in the tenth grade after Mrs. Johnson had passed and they were no longer being home schooled. Sophia's long, dark hair and beautiful blue eyes had been the object of his dreams for months.

Earl held the flowers he had bought firmly, lilies -her favorite-along with a box of chocolates. He had gotten them with all of his allowances, and he could not tell which chocolate brand she liked, so he got her the kind without the nuts in them.

He liked to believe he knew everything about her. After all, he had learned all about her by breaking into her locker and stealing her diary. He was sure to return it before school started the next day, so she had not missed it. In fact, Sophia had not even suspected a thing. Earl remembered thinking that he liked nuts, but Sophia did not, which was a good contrast. He had wanted to impress the girl he loved.

At that time, Earl thought he knew she loved him too. She showed him her love in the way she smiled at him every day. Sometimes, he would see her with that Ken guy, but he was very confident that Ken was only a distraction and that in the end, he would be out of the picture while he and Sophia would have a happily ever after.

Earl had skipped his classes that day and hid under the bleachers in the gym. That was his favorite place to hide whenever he did not want to be in class or when he did not want to be around people. Kids could be cruel, especially the guys on the football team. They always teased and made fun of him. Earl tried not to let it get to him but sometimes, it got unbearable. Earl made himself feel better by imagining their heads explode, all that blood and brain matter raining down on him as the others fled in terror. It put a smile on his face.

Today, however, this hiding place served a different purpose. He hid there because he knew Sophia would be having gym class soon and he wanted to see her. The second bell rang, and the gym soon filled up like the other students showed up for an hour; he watched Sophia and the other cheerleaders practice. She was so beautiful and lithe and athletic. Everything he could wish for in a girl.

The jocks were also there; they were always there. Earl remembered them throwing balls around and acting like they were better than everyone else. He never liked throwing balls, nor did he like any jocks. Somehow, someone always hit him in the head with one. Earl could also see Ken watching Sophia. The memory made his blood boil, but all he did was watch. After all, Sophia loved him and only him.

They were in the same class. Sophia was his best friend in the world, and nothing could change that.

Earl remembered the sensation that followed as the last bell rang. It was exhilarating, and he could feel the blood pumping through his veins. It was show time. He took a deep breath, getting ready to express his love to Sophia in front of the whole world. He stepped out from behind the bleachers just as the cheerleaders were packing up to hit the showers.

One... Two... Three... Four... Five... Six... Seven...
One... Two... Three... Four... Five... Six... Seven...

He counted in his head as he took his approach a step at a time, tapping his thigh as he went. Seven... oddly, counting to seven always seemed to calm him down. First his right, then his left. The chocolates and flowers he held made it hard to tap his thighs as he walked but he managed somehow.

"Sophia!" He called at the top of his voice; his lips stretched in a large smile. Sophia looked up from where she had bent over to pick up her gym bag. Her face lit up with a smile when she spotted Earl in the middle of the gym. Her smile was not as bright as it normally was, but he figured she was tired from all the jumping and cheerleading she had done.

Sophia flipped her long black hair to her back, and he could see the color flood her cheeks from excitement. He knew she was just as happy about this as he was or at least he thought she was. Sophia was very tired; he was the last thing on her mind. The whole gym went silent, everyone was shocked at first but then they began to murmur and chuckle at Earl and Sophia's expense. Earl did not care though; he was kind of expecting it from them.

'Who is the weirdo?' 'Look at this twerp!' 'Look like someone's lost it'- he heard them loud and clear. Earl had expected this. None of them knew what it meant to truly be in love, so Earl let them say what they pleased. They were unimportant; all that mattered was Sophia and his love for her.

"I heard Sophia say he would not leave her alone, always following her around like a lost puppy and she could not get rid of him." Earl heard a girl whisper as he approached Sophia. Smiling ignorantly as he did.

One... Two... Three...

He counted louder in his head to drown out their voices.

...Four... Five... Six... Seven...

He noticed they had stepped aside so he could talk to Sophia; as annoying as they were, he appreciated them for that much. They either looked at him dirty because they were jealous or frowned at him as though he were a thing to pity. 'Pity... why would I need their pity?' He remembered asking himself.

As far as he was concerned, Sophia loved that he was brave enough to put up such a display for her. He was wrong. She had her back to him the entire time and when she did turn to face him, her eyes lit up, but not in the way he liked.

They were irritating her. That had to be the only reason she would be so crossed; she was mad at them for being so ignorant and rude with the nonsense they whispered loudly. He and Sophia were not official yet, but he was working on fixing that and then they would be together after he asked her out. Earl walked closer to where Sophia was and stopped directly in front of her.

He smiled up at her, sure that his smile would entice her but that was not the case. Sophia's eyes were sharp with a glare, and she was embarrassed and furious. Earl had never seen her so mad, but he was not expecting her to do what she did next.

"You! Of course, it's you!" She snapped. "What do you think you are doing?"

Earl was surprised but did not talk. He had not expected this. He shook his head and handed her the flowers and chocolate. Their voices had ticked her off; if his smile could not do the trick, then his gifts had to. Earl was sure. She just needed to be reminded of how much they loved each other. What they muttered about them meant nothing to them. She loved him, did she not?

She refused to take either of them and slapped them out of his hand instead. An incident flashed through his mind. A week ago, Sophia had been acting strange, but he had chalked it up to the stress of applying to colleges.

As usual, he had been walking with her after school when she suddenly turned on him and screamed.

"Leave me the hell alone, weirdo!" Sophia grabbed by his collar with both her fists balled. "Fuck off and stop following me around!"

"So... S-Sophia" He gasped in shock as he tried to calm her down, but she shoved him to the floor as everyone watched and cooed in awe like it was some sort of show. Earl was petrified and stared up at her in horror as tears welled up in his eyes. Everyone laughed at him, but that did not matter to Earl. Something was wrong with Sophia; this was not like her. How could Sophia do this to him? Did she not know he loved her?

...Four... Five... Six... Seven...

Granted, he had never told her, but she could see his love for her in his eyes. Right?

"... Why're you being mean to me. I thought you knew?"

Earl could not bring himself to look her in the eye, but Sophia's sweet face had morphed into one of contempt.

"Knew what?!" Sophia hissed, "You're a fucking weirdo! I would never be with you. Give me my fucking space! Stop creeping all over the place and enough with the smiling- I am not your friend!"

She stomped over his flowers and chocolates and then stormed out of the gym crying. In her absence, laughter erupted from everyone who watched, and it was laughter that rang in his ears for days after that incident. All Earl could do was lay there and cry.

…One… Two… Three… Four… Five… Six… Seven… Seven… Seven… Seven…

Earl could not move. Like a lion's roar, a loud sound sounded in his ears. It felt like his head was going to explode.

"You loser!" Kyle Sanders, one of the footballers and Ken's friends walked up to him.

"What made you think you could have her?" He asked laughing in Earl's face and kicking him on the floor. Earl groaned; the pain Kyle caused made him hate him so much more than he already did. He hated all. He hated them all so much that he wished they would die horrible deaths. He wished he had his father's gun again.

…Seven… Seven… Seven…

Earl clawed at his ears. Seven… he saw it. Everyone thought he was crying because he was sad or in pain, but it was none of that. He was not as simple-minded as they were. He had seen something horrible; it was Sophia. When she said those awful things, he understood that she was not herself, but he saw it still. Just above her eyes was the number seven. She was marked, tainted…EVIL.

He remained on the floor in the middle of the gym, crying among what was left of his gifts. Everyone left and so he cried. His heart ached and he felt betrayed. The janitor came in and met him there. Seeing him, Earl thought the man must have chuckled and muttered something under his breath. He was no different from all the others that Earl hated- disgusting.

Then he heard it—Duke's laugh.

"I told you not to do it. She never loved us. You are a pathetic, sorry loser. You're just like your mother. Weak..naive... spineless!" Duke said, still laughing.

Duke was his friend sometimes, and this was not one of those times.

"Shut up!" Earl screamed and balled his fists so hard he could feel his nails moments away from breaking flesh. The janitor looked back at him and then walked back to the middle of the gym where Earl lay.

"Are you alright, boy? Who are you talking to?" The man asked. Earl looked at him wanting to grab the man by his ugly moustache, only to have the satisfaction of seeing someone else in pain. When he did not answer, the man looked at him with pity in his eyes. He tried to help Earl up, but Earl refused.

"You go home, boy. You'll feel better in the morning." He said and walked away.

'Poor thing's gone crazy.' Earl heard the man whisper under his breath as he left.

He was not crazy.

"Yes, you are," Duke said. ***"You're crazy to have thought a girl like Sophia would be in love with us."***

Earl shook his head from left to right. He always had to do things like this if he wanted Duke to quiet down and leave him alone.

Duke was quiet when he had shaken his head seven times. Earl got up, picked up his abandoned school bag and walked out of the gym, thankful that everyone else had been long gone by that time of day, and he did not have to endure any awkward gazes on his way home.

That night, Earl secluded himself in the woods behind his house. It was one of the few places he did not feel estranged. He sat in a tree; anywhere was better than home. It was too filled with too much grief for his already broken heart to bear. He did not want to talk with his foster father. The house was somber from all the loss they had endured. They had lost both Sarah, his foster sister, and Mrs. Johnson. Sarah had tried to carry out an abortion and had died while Mrs. Johnson had passed from grief and ill health. Molly was still crying while Neil was always sulking and snapping at everyone.

Earl went through the rest of high school being pointed at as the boy who Sophia rejected. Funny, the harder he tried to forget her the more reminded of her he got. His classmates were the worst, and he hated all of them, and if he got his way, then they would all die violent deaths. He hated Sophia the most- And Ken and Kyle.

"If wishes were horses..." Duke whispered in his ears.

"Leave me alone, Duke..."

"I've told you what needs to be done, but you refuse to listen."

Earl shook his head and began counting again. He had made a lot of stupid decisions in his life but even he could tell doing anything Duke asked of him would be the height of it.

IT WAS NOT A FOND MEMORY BUT NOW THAT EARL LOOKED back at it, it did not hurt as much as it used to. Earl watched her take the stairs two at a time, and he was happy to see her. He still felt like the boy he was back in high school. She had rejected him then, but he did not hate her for it. It was not her fault; he was more relieved to see that the number had left her. It was a memory that haunted him, but now he shrugged at it. He was naive and they were too young. People change.

Obviously, it had been ten years since they graduated High school; hardly anyone remembered that day as vividly as he did. Some people remembered though. Those who did still made fun of him, but Earl was mature enough to ignore them. He understood that there was no point in holding petty grudges because if he let himself hate them… then he would hate her too. He did not want to hate Sophia.

"Well, your opportunity has come. This is our chance… let's do what we've always wanted to do." Duke's raspy voice sounded in his ear. For some reason, Duke's wicked tone sounded happy rather than disdainful for once- Earl did not like it. Earl heard the voice loud and clear, and it was a voice in his head. He could not ignore it even if he tried. He began to count as he turned to leave.

One… Two…

*"**Before you hide me away, why don't you hear me out for once?**"* Duke asked.

…Four… Five…

Earl stopped in the middle of counting but continued to tap his thigh.

*"**They say love is blind… but you're no fool. You need to do something about her. I mean, she couldn't even remember our name, and besides, she already has the mark on her forehead.**"*

"It's gone; I didn't see it-." He whispered.

*"**You didn't see it? Or you just didn't want to?**"*

He had noticed that she still had the number seven on her forehead. Duke was not easy to fool. "What would you have me do?"

*"**Something simple. You just sit back and let me take over.**"* Duke replied.

Earl froze in his tracks. "Bullshit!" he exclaimed loudly, "You can't do that."

*"**I can do a lot of things you don't know. If only you'd let me show you,**"* Duke said, his voice soft and tempting. It made Earl wonder if such a thing were possible. Could Duke truly take the reins to his body? What would Duke do with him? - Earl grimaced; he could not believe he was even considering it. So, he began to count.

*"**Listen to me… Can you hear me? Shut up!**"* Duke roared, his voice so loud it made Earl's ears sting as he fell to his knees. *"**I've had enough of your stupidity, you fucking coward. You're making a**"*

fool of us, let me take care of this once and for all- YOU NEED ME."

"No! I can't." Earl said, his voice weakening.

"That's why you have me. I'll do what needs to be done- Now shut the hell up and let me out!" Duke commanded.

Earl wanted to protest; he tried to count, to struggle- but it was all in vain. He choked and spasmed with his eyes rolled back as a new sensation wafted over him. It was sinister and cold yet oddly familiar. He felt as though two hands were clutching down his throat, seizing his vocal cord and claiming his voice. The same sensation stung his ears, eyes, legs, and even his hands until just as abruptly as the pain began, it seized and he was laying on the floor. The pain was gone, but so was Earl. In his place stood a man with a smile so sinister one would believe it was smiling up from the pits of hell. Duke was in charge now.

He had walked a good distance from Sophia's apartment building, but he turned and could see it clear as day.

I AM BACK!!!

CHAPTER

TWO

Earl woke up in a chipper mood. He fixed himself breakfast, whistling while he dressed up. The other guy preferred to get coffee from the diner downstairs.

He rummaged through a chest of drawers in his kitchen until he found a rolled-up plastic bag. He grinned, already anticipating the thrill. He opened the bag and laid it up on the counter, careful not to spill any. He brought a piece of paper and poured some of the powder from the plastic bag onto the paper, ensuring the paper was in a perfect line. He bent his nose close to the paper and snorted.

"Ahh…" He said, raising his head. Bliss. Pure, unadulterated cocaine.

Now he could get started with his day. First of all, breakfast.

This Earl, Duke if you will, preferred home-cooked meals. He especially loved steak but always had to eat pancakes because they were Earl's favorite. At least he was always generous with the syrup.

He had always wondered why the other guy chose to call him Duke. Maybe because his own name was Earl. So, both names were titles in England. He shrugged and laughed at his own analysis.

The cocaine made him think deep thoughts, making it harder for Earl to nag him. Duke laughed out loud.

He decided they were going to have pancakes with the extra syrup this morning. Duke poured himself a glass of orange juice and drank it all in one gulp. He quickly fixed himself breakfast from scratch. None of that packaged mix for him. Good old flour, eggs, and milk.

He sat down at the small dining table to sit, swinging his legs as he did, like a child who had just been given his favorite toys. He loved when he could come out to play- through this could barely count as playing. The other guy was much too timid, and watching the world through his eyes was awfully boring.

It was a beautiful day, and he thought as he looked out the window.

The other guy was spineless and a wimp, Duke thought. He would not be able to do what he needed to do. It was the work of the Chosen. He wondered how anyone would think Earl was capable of doing the work he had been chosen to do. Anyway, that was why Duke had been sent to help Earl. He liked being in charge better.

He also wondered how one person could be two completely different people within the same body. One time he took control and decided to get some reading done. He wanted to believe that the other guy was merely a figment of his imagination but in the end, he was left to realize one thing. 'I, Duke, and Earl, the other guy, are not the same,' not that he cared. What he knew was that they had an assignment to carry out. The other guy would be the face everyone knew and loved while he would be the one who did the dirty work.

He did not mind the dirty work either.

Most times, Earl was allowed to live his life the way he wanted but sometimes, taking over the host was necessary. Times like this.

Right now, Duke was the real one. He did not like to consider themselves as personalities; they were more than that, distinct- special. Trying to explain this to himself was giving him a headache. He gave up. All he knew was that Earl was in there. Somewhere. Probably whimpering and sucking on his thumb. He chuckled at the image.

After breakfast, he cleaned the dishes and the counter, ensuring he could see his reflection on the countertop.

He arranged all the pots, pans, and bottles at a 7-degree angle. Everything had to be just so, or Earl would have a meltdown when he returned, and Duke couldn't have that.

Duke walked out of the apartment, locked it up behind him and set out. He quickly stashed the plastic bag of cocaine into his pocket, and he would need some at some point during the day. He turned the lock first three times then back another three times. Then he turned it one last time. That was how Earl had to do it. Everything in sevens.

Seven pairs of shoes. Seven shirts and seven pants. Seven pairs of socks. Even his furniture was arranged in a way to form the number seven.

Earl's phone rang. Mr. Johnson. Duke shook his head and did not pick up the call. Mr. Johnson had a good heart. At least he treated them better than Earl's biological father had, but the man was holding them back. He was not allowing him to live to his full potential. Always on him to take those damn medications and be good. The medications that Duke was sure to dispose of.

It was annoying. The medications made them drowsy and difficult to think clearly. Good thing Earl had conveniently 'forgotten' to take them last night and accidentally threw them out in the morning.

Jim Harris from work called and Bertha too. It was amusing to Duke seeing how all of them loved Earl. And that was because of him, Duke was sure. The other guy had never been confident in his life, having his self-esteem battered first by his father, then by every child in high school. Somehow, the other guy exuded Earl's confidence at work so much that his co-workers liked him and respected him. Respect. Earl owed Duke respect.

That was all he ever wanted. Respect.

Crest Hill was a small town, and one could easily walk from one end of the town to the other. It took Duke less than thirty minutes to get to where he was going. He entered the tiny bookstore run by Mrs. Golding. The door made a tiny tinkling sound as its bell rang when he opened it, and he hated the sound.

"Welcome. Make yourself comfortable." She said as he entered.

Duke found a couch that allowed him to look out the window at the entrance to the apartment building opposite the bookshop. The couch was placed in such a way that no one could see him, but he could see everyone who came into the bookstore and even those outside. The perfect seat for a stakeout.

The other guy would have walked to the counter and exchanged pleasantries with the old woman, and today was not a day for pleasantries. Thankfully, the woman was near-blind but would never wear her glasses, so she could not see who had come in.

She also did not have any cameras installed so he was safe. Even if she did, Duke was confident in his abilities. He chuckled, wondering how the woman remained in business. Duke was surprised she had not been robbed blind yet, but people had a healthy respect for Mrs. Golding, and no one dared steal from her or tried to mug her even though she was eighty years old and practically blind. She hired an assistant, but he only came on weekends. He was a student.

He even liked the woman, and she had grit.

Duke watched the entrance for almost two hours, and she did not come out. He had packed the rest of his breakfast so he would not get hungry. Duke was patient and since he was not standing in anyone's way, he had the whole day to wait.

Being someone who most people largely ignored had taught him patience. The perks of being the weirdo no one wanted.

He knew there was no other entrance or exit to the apartment building. Everyone would have to come out or go in through those same doors, and he was watching.

Finally, she came out of the apartment, still wearing her sleeping clothes at about six P.M. in the evening. What a waste of humanity, Duke thought in contempt.

But damn! She was still charming, even though she looked tired. The glowing mark on her forehead did not take anything out of her beauty but it strengthened his resolve. Duke was glad he was in control, and the other guy would have softened up and given up on doing the needful.

It was all very simple. The number seven symbolized evil and that's all he needed to know. Anyone or anything on whom the sign appeared was meant to die. If they were not killed, someone in Earl's life would die. They had been chosen to do this important task in order to save the lives of Earl's loved ones.

Duke immediately got up and left the bookstore, following Sophia inconspicuously from a distance. Once his sights were locked, there was no escaping Duke. It was still light, although the sun was already setting. People were still about the street but none of that mattered to him. He had become her shadow, but she would be too ignorant to notice him. It was only a matter of time and soon, it would be dark enough for him to work.

He pulled the bill of his hat down, obscuring his face. He walked behind Sophia, following her without being detected. She walked into a grocery store and Duke followed her in.

Duke made sure to stay clear of all the cameras but was still sure to have her within his sights as he stalked her. The store was small enough for him to do that. She picked up a pack of cigarettes, paid for them, and walked out of the store. She lit one when she stepped outside the store and took in a deep puff, closing her eyes as she inhaled. She let out her breath.

Sophia was startled when she opened her eyes, and he was in front of her. He raised the bill of his hat a bit, allowing her to see his face.

"Oh! It's you." She said, placing her hand on her chest. Her face showed that she was relieved, although she was not excited to see him. Duke smiled at her, watching as she let her guard down and become relaxed.

Duke was not amused by her reaction, but he was expecting it. Just what he wanted. He wanted her to think she was safe with him; Earl had already done a lousy job at that, so he was almost certain she would be conscious of him. He put his hand in his pants pocket, striking a non-threatening pose. For once, looking like Earl and behaving like him was actually useful. He fingered the chisel he had placed in his pocket just before leaving the apartment.

"Hey, Sophia. I didn't know you smoked." Duke said to her in Earl's gentle voice, a shy smile on his face. He could see her becoming more relaxed.

"We keep running into each other. If I didn't know any better, I would have thought you were following me or something." Sophia said, laughing. She still held her lit cigarette between her forefinger and middle finger. He could hear a hint of suspicion in her voice, but he just shrugged.

"I work around here, and I was on my way back home and just stopped to get some groceries when I saw you." He explained. This seemed to assuage her suspicion as she continued to smoke.

"Don't be silly. Town's too small for all that."

"Good point," She shrugged with a grin.

"It's good to see you again after all this while. Was almost convinced last night was a dream."

"Oh please… I bet you've got better things to dream about."

"I mean it. How have you been?" He asked as he fell in step with her.

"So-so, I guess. Are you not going to buy anything?" She asked, looking pointedly at his empty hands. Duke still had his hat low over his face, so he could not be recognized by others passing by.

"Nah…I came out for a stroll. Thought of getting a few beers, though but remembered I already had some at home," He scoffed. Sophia nodded, it sounded believable enough and she bought his story.

"Why don't we head over to the park and catch up? It has been what…ten years? It has been so long." Duke said softly. Sophia paused staring at him intently, and he could see her internal struggle; Duke could tell he was pushing his luck, but he had noticed the last time that she was troubled. She must have been running away from something at home and because of it, she did not hesitate as much as he thought she would.

"Yeah, sure. What the heck!" she said as she joined him. Duke smiled internally, her actions were more driven by guilt than hospitality and he knew it but that did not matter. The results would be the same either way.

The park was a block away from her apartment and had a few metal benches on which people could sit and relax. They had umbrellas for sunny days. Duke had chosen that park purposely. It was a wide-open space, enough to keep her relaxed. It was also rather quiet and away from the main path. The sun was already setting at the time, and it would soon be dark.

She was relaxed, 'Why wouldn't she be?'

Everything was going as Duke had planned. This was not going to be like Earl's childish love confession ten years ago, and Duke had covered all his bases.

He gently steered her to the bench furthest from the road and closest to a grove of trees. She had not noticed anything particular, but Duke had his reasons. This grove was the same one the students used to hang out at while they were in high school. The school was on the other side of the grove. The story of a woman found dead in the woods had caused people to abandon the path. But the grove becoming off limits was just what he needed.

Duke knew the path very well and could even walk through it in the dark. He remembered times when they had needed to escape, and this grove had been the best place to hide. As they approached it, he wondered what he had done to get her so chatty; if Earl were conscious, he would have been jealous, but Duke was in the mood for none of it.

He looked around to make sure no one was in sight as he listened to her incessant rants. Just as she was about to sit down, Duke raised his hand and landed a blow to her temple, knocking her out cold. He paused. 'That's it?' Duke thought bewilderedly and feared he would have needed to do that twice or more to knock her out, yet there she lay, unconscious. He looked around again just to be sure. One could not be too careful. Everything had to go as planned and an audience was not part of his plans. At least not now.

He gently lifted Sophia's limp body to his shoulder. It felt like she weighed nothing. Thanks to his days on the Johnson farm, Earl had lost a whole lot of weight and gained enough muscle strength. He made sure to keep fit, paying for gym memberships that he knew Earl would not refuse. Earl loved to shut him out, but Duke always got his way. He moved effortlessly through the small path in the woods. It was a five-minute walk and Duke had not even broken a sweat.

It made sense that things would end where it had all started. There was a large oak tree, similar to the one on the farm where Earl had grown up with his parents before going to live with the Johnsons.

Earlier, he had bought a new rope and stashed it in his small pouch. He stripped her of her clothes, leaving her naked. He looked down at her as she lay naked and unconscious; her naked body did nothing for him. He had no desire to have sex with her. Instead, he grimaced at the thought that a lump of meat such as herself had wrong him. He carefully folded the clothes and kept them in a zip lock bag he had brought along with him.

A souvenir or trophy if you will. He knew it was cliché, but he had to have something to remember this night by.

He tied Sophia to the large tree with the rope, careful not to touch her directly. He had watched enough movies to know they could trace a person by bodily fluids. He wore gloves and his entire body covered to avoid scratching against any surface and leaving any body fluids behind him. He kept his hair closely shaved in a buzz cut and did not need to worry about any being found at the crime scene.

Duke made sure to run the rope around her in seven loops and tied her off with a seven knot. He took out his small camera and snapped her. Sophia did not look as beautiful as she had in high school or even earlier when she had been awake.

He brought out a lipstick he had in his pants pocket. He was glad he had brought it along. He had not known he would need this and had only picked it up at the store on a whim, not even paying for it. He lifted her head with his gloved hand and gently applied the lipstick to her lips. He liked the color. Blood red. The color stood out starkly against her white face. Fitting.

Now it was time to wait. He wanted her to be awake. While he was waiting, he fortified himself with his cocaine.

After about ten minutes, Sophia began to stir. She slowly regained her consciousness and immediately began to struggle against the rope as it bit into her.

"Welcome back," Duke said in his raspy voice.

Sophia gasped and yelled for help, but he smiled and watched her intently. He did not make a move to stop or silence her, and he let her yell and cry; when satisfied, he walked up to her. "Done yet? Good"

He struck her across the face, blowing her so hard he knocked a tooth out and laughed.

"Why are you doing this to me?" She asked, her voice panicked. She squinted when he shone the light directly into her face. She did not recognize his voice and was convinced someone had kidnapped Earl and her.

She was such a drama queen. The light was not that bright Duke thought, rolling his eyes.

"What I should have done a long time ago," Duke said, pulling out the chisel from his pocket. The sun had set behind the mountain in the distance. There was a soft glow over Crest Hill, but he still needed the light. He placed the light in his headband and covered it with some tape, dimming the light a bit. He walked closer to Sophia. She looked at him with wide eyes, and he liked the look in her eyes.

'I know what you're thinking," he smirked, "Surprise…"

"Why are you doing this to me?" She groaned, seeing his intent, she asked him, a pleading tone creeping into her voice.

"I have to silly; you wouldn't get it" He sighed, "No one is going to hear your screams but having you scream in my ears would be counterproductive," Duke said calmly. Sophia was already nodding her head, promising to be quiet. Her jaw stung; getting hit again was the last thing on her mind.

"Why are you doing this? We've known each other for a long time, or you can't still be mad about high school." She said, her mind scrambling for an explanation.

When she brought up high school, Duke saw red and struck her across the face again, so hard her neck jerked, and he feared it had snapped.

"Jeez… hehe," He gasped. "Look what you made me do. A sec there, I thought I'd killed you" Duke laughed, seeing the red mark across her face. He had not planned to touch her face. He gently caressed her face, and he had broken her nose. "You should not have brought that incident up. It's still quite a sore spot, you know. He was truly in love with you, and I could not get over you either. I thought we were friends."

"You… you never spoke." She winced and coughed, "… to me. Until that day! We never spoke, and you followed me around and I found that creep …um … uncomfortable." She quickly amended.

"Well… Earl was an idiot. I guess that was his fault."

Sophia was railing, she found herself panting and the taste of her own blood clung to her tongue. "I'm sorry," Sophia muttered incessantly like a broken record, scrambling for more time. "…I'll do anything."

She's lying. All she does is lie.

"Of course, you will do and say anything. You have no choice right now. But you don't have anything I want any longer. You are just a despicable little slut. I wonder what we saw in you all those years." Duke said as she broke down in tears.

"We?" She asked, looking around to see if there were more people in the trees. Sophia thought it was despicable, she was scared but even then, she wanted to know who else was doing this. Duke ignored her, as hard as it was to believe he understood that she was concussed and confused.

"What I would like to know now is this. How far would you go to save your own life?" He asked, pausing for effect. He had called her a drama queen, but Duke loved to make things interesting.

"Please… anything. I'm sorry," Sophia pleaded.

"Then I'll ask a question. Get it right… and I'll patch you right up; how does that sound?"

Sophia hesitated but nodded and he clapped loudly, startling her as he did.

"What's my name?" He asked and knelt close to her, looking directly into her face. Terror could not fully describe what she felt. Confusion crept into her eyes and Duke was infuriated by how beautiful despair looked on her. So beautiful, he was tempted to take her head home with him.

"You don't even remember my name!" He shouted, spittle flying out of the corners of his mouth and landing on her face. He was more of a wild animal bearing its fangs than a man.

"You humiliated me all those years ago, called me names, and yet you don't remember my name."

"I'm sorry," she cried desperately with her eyes shut. The pain, the cold, the fear… even if he were to spare her, he had broken her already. Not that he had any intentions of doing so.

"All we wanted was for you to accept our love." His voice trailed off in sadness, the only indication that the other guy was still there.

Sophia was shaking violently, tears pouring down the sides of her face and snot from her broken nose. He looked at her now and struggled to see the beauty that had so bewitched Earl in her.

He had to move back to calm himself. If he allowed himself to act in anger, he would not be able to revel in what he would do next, which would defeat his purpose.

Duke was going to make her pay for his sadness with sorrow and he intended to enjoy every moment of it. He needed to calm down and did not want to kill her earlier than she needed to die. He took deep breaths and calmed himself. He moved closer to her, drew out a new handkerchief, and wiped her face. He could not leave any trace of himself on her.

He checked the knot again to make sure her hands remained tied to her back. He made sure it was very tight, allowing the rope to bite into the skin of her arms and send dribbles of blood trailing down her wrists. All and all, it was a beautiful sight to behold and he was proud of himself.

Right now, he felt like a satiated lion playing with its prey. He had played with his food long enough, and it was time to get into action. Duke pulled out the chisel from his pocket. He heard Sophia's quick intake of breath and smiled with delight.

"Let us see how much you would have left once your beauty is gone." He said and quickly stuffed her open mouth with a new handkerchief before she could scream. Now that he was ready to work, he did not want her distracting him with her annoying pleas and deafening cries.

Using the chisel, he forced it down through her flesh and slowly carved out the number 7 on her forehead, relishing the feel meat as it was torn to release a steady flow of blood. He enjoyed that she had enough fight in her to squirm and flail as he toyed with her. He was careful though, and he did not want her ending her torment by his hands with the chisel held out and was glad that thanks to the handkerchief in her mouth, she could not bite off her tongue, though the thought did cross her mind. She jerked and twisted, causing the rope to dig deeper into her skin. The harder she struggled, the deeper the dry handkerchief slid down her mouth, suffocating her.

Duke stopped; breaking her nose was a mistake; had he not removed the gag when he did, she would have died from it. He paused and watched her draw some breath.

"Please… stop. I am sorry. I am so sorry." She sobbed. The other guy would have been satisfied with her apology. But she deserved to die and that was why he was doing this not Earl. Earl was too soft.

"Sorry, it does not cut it, Sophia. You had your chance and can remember me forever in the afterlife. Remember Earl Hughes." He said as he stuffed the gag back on and resumed his task. She was a hag to him, but he was determined to make a masterpiece out of her, though he had barely finished the first figure when she passed out from the pain.

She had lost a lot of blood as it was, but it was none of Duke's concern. He sat on the ground when he finished what he considered to be a work of art. He surveyed her face, enjoying how the smell of blood had overcome her scent. It poured down her forehead unto her face and chest.

When he was satisfied with what he saw, Duke brought out the piece of twine he had brought along and stood behind the tree. His arms could easily reach around the trunk, and he placed the twine like a garrote around the woman's throat and pulled with all his strength.

Soon enough, her body began to twist and jerk. Duke could feel her struggle for breath. He pulled and twisted until he felt the life drain out of her. It was done; she was dead.

The feeling was like nothing any drug could do for him. Duke felt a high that reminded him of doing the same things to the small animals on his father's farm. The feeling of having power over another creature.

This was not going to end just like this. Sophia's death was a statement. He freed the body from the tree, wiped it clean of most of the now thick blood and dragged it to the edge grove closest to school. He propped her up against the tree beside the school's side entrance, her hands folded between her crossed legs. He brought out his small camera and took several pictures. Knowing all too well that Earl would try to repress the memory of their work without the proof there to remind him.

Anyone who saw her from afar would think she had just fallen asleep.

Soon, Crest Hill would be awake, and they would see what he had done for them. They would be grateful for what he had just helped them be rid of.

"You are welcome." He whispered under his breath and chuckled.

He left a note for the police, and it was never complete without a note.

Some would not appreciate his work, and he was sure many could call him a monster, evil, or mad. They were wrong, and he was none of those things. Duke did not feel like any of those things. Instead, Duke felt like God.

He felt he had a purpose for the first time in a long time.

EARL WOKE UP WITH A SPLITTING HEADACHE. HE HAD forgotten to take his medication again last night. He needed to watch it as it was beginning to occur more often these days. It never happened when he had been staying with the Johnsons. Mrs. Johnson always made sure he took them. God rest her soul.

Earl had a feeling he was missing something. He could not rightly remember how he had gotten home the day before. Come to think of it, and he could barely remember anything that had happened. He strolled over to the cabinet over his sink where his pills were supposed to be, but they were gone. He paused. Earl strolled back to the table by his bed and had stashed a few of his meds there too- they were also gone. His heart began to pound. It felt like a ticking time bomb. Something was not right, and Earl could feel it to his bones.

He scrambled about his room when he realized just how clean it was. No… the room was too clean. It was never a mess but now it had this air about it as though someone else had been moving his stuff and cleaning after him. His feet felt sore. Earl was confused. He hurried into the kitchen and was glad to mind some of his meds hidden behind a box of cereal- he remembered putting them there one time but being too lazy to get them out. He was about to take them when he noticed the floors had been mopped clean. Whoever had done it, was in a hurry. As he investigated, he found his shoes. Leaves and mulch were stuck to it. Earl was dumbfounded. To the best of his knowledge, he had not gone into the woods.

What happened yesterday?

His eyes felt sore as he rubbed his eyes with the heel of his palm. He sat with his elbows on his knees and held his head. The last time he had a bad headache was when his mother left him, and it was the day the police had taken her away.

Earl shook his head and immediately regretted it. He slowly got up, careful not to shake his head anymore. He felt like he was having a hangover but knew that was not possible. Earl seldom drank any alcohol, and he had his biological father to thank for that. The man had put the fear of alcohol in Earl.

His stomach heaved and bile rose up to his throat. He quickly went to sink, and he was barely at the sink when his stomach emptied out its contents. After puking his guts out, he washed his face and leaned heavily on the sink.

He slowly walked back to his bed and checked for his phone. Ten missed calls, and most from his boss at work and Mr. Johnson. He looked at the time, and it was 7 A.M on Thursday.

Thursday? How can it be Thursday? Hadn't yesterday been Tuesday?

"What happened?" He muttered to himself. The last thing he remembered was meeting Sophia on Tuesday night at the High School and walking her home, and meeting her had dredged up the old emotions of her rejection.

He looked at his phone again. The date was the same. He had lost time. An entire day to be precise. Had I slept through it? He wondered.

He went to the sink, filled a glass with water from the tap, and took a deep gulp. Still holding his phone and the glass, he walked to the small center table in his equally small room and turned the television on.

His apartment was small, but Earl was rather proud of it. It was the first sign of his independence. He could walk the length and breadth of the room in seven strides which was very convenient for when he got agitated.

His center table was set at an odd angle but that was how Earl liked it. In fact, the whole room was arranged in an odd way. Odd to any ordinary person, and that was why he never had guests over.

He flicked on the television, slowly lowering himself into the sofa. The news was on.

"…the naked body of a woman in her late twenties was found in the woods surrounding the Crest Hill High School. Police say the body was found by a young teenager who had been on his way to school but has not been able to identify the body yet. First responders at the scene say the…" The reporter's voice faded as a roaring sound filled Earl's ears.

"No… no…" Earl whispered, knowing exactly what happened. Suddenly the whole day he had missed came rushing back. It was almost like something happening to another person. He felt like he had come out of his body and watched someone else do all that Duke…he had done to Sophia.

Earl was disgusted and he ran back to the sink and puked again, his stomach and chest heaving in tandem.

"What have you done?" He whispered to no one in particular, and Duke was silent.

Earl began to shake; his entire body began to vibrate. He held his hands out in front of him and suddenly, he could smell the strong stench of iron. 'Please!!!!' her voice bellowed startling Earl to the floor panting.

Everything- Earl remembered everything. He remembered the feeling of Sophia's life draining out of her as he had strangled her with the twine. He remembered the blood and horror and the fear in her eyes.

Worse was he remembered enjoying her suffering.

"No… N-no NO!" He panicked. "What have you done?"

He was still standing over the sink. Furious. The rage was burning in his eyes as he glared at his reflection. "What did you do!" Earl asked again, louder this time.

He watched in dazed horror as the rage in his eyes waned into an exasperated scowl and his reflection smiled back at him smugly. ***"Quit being a bitch… you knew I was going to do this,"*** Duke responded this time.

"Oh god… you killed her- We killed her"

"This is the higher calling to which you have been called. I have been telling you this for years, but you wouldn't fucking listen. Did you really think it ended with HER?" He said, his raspy voice taking on a delighted tone.

Earl crumpled to the floor as his legs gave way. Tears began to roll down his cheeks until he began to bawl. He crawled to his bed, his legs unable to carry him, and he remained on the floor with his back to the bed.

Earl shifted and his hands encountered something under the bed. He pulled a plastic bag out from under the bed, and there were clothes inside. He opened the bag and caught a whiff of incense.

He slowly recognized what they were and whose they were. Duke had brought Sophia's clothes home with him. Earl dropped the bag like they were hot, got up on unsteady legs, and began to pace the room.

One... Two... Three... Four... Five... Six... Seven...

Then he turned in the opposite direction.

"What am I going to do now?" He asked himself, looking down at his hands. He vaguely remembered his mother asking the same question when his father had died.

...One... Two... Three...

He counted as he crawled, trying to calm himself down.

His hands were shaking. How could he have forgotten to take his medications? He believed Duke about being the Chosen but had never imagined that Duke would actually take it this far.

When it was just small animals, it was still acceptable. No one missed them. But a human being. A person with families who would miss them. His father did not count. The man was an animal, and he deserved what he got.

'And the police!' Earl's eyes grew wide when he realized that an investigation would be held.

...Four... Five...

"Relax, I took care of everything. No one would trace anything to us." Duke said, chuckling. Earl sighed in relief but immediately became agitated again. Even though Duke was meticulous, and Earl trusted him, it did not make what he had done acceptable.

"That still does not make it okay to kill people," Earl said, with less conviction in his voice.

"You know she had to die. She had the mark on her." Duke retorted, already sounding annoyed.

…Six… Seven…

He picked up the small camera he had bought on a whim some time ago and began to look through the photos. Images of Sophia's dead body jumped up at him. Earl welled up in disgust and cried. He really loved her, now he was conflicted. He was sorry for her, and no one deserved to die such a death. He could hear her cries in his head, and he remembered how afraid she was, how she had cried and begged him- how it felt to snuff her. It was exhilarating. Earl was disgusted by himself.

"That's it. Remember that. Remember how much power we had." Duke said as Earl flung the camera across the room and began to count out loud this time. He had felt helpless for too long in his life, and now, he did not know how to feel.

Nonetheless, Duke was not done. Not by a long shot.

EARL DRESSED UP EXTRA CAREFULLY THAT MORNING AND prepared to go to work. Every fiber in his body wanted to stay home, to keep Duke away from the light of day but he was not going to let himself cower from Duke. He was going to treat himself to a big breakfast, not that he deserved any of it. Work was draining, but he needed the money. He glared at the small mirror above his chest of drawers as he knotted his tie. Knowing Duke could be watching through his eyes put him on edge.

No medications today again. He feared the ones he had hid had gone bad, but he hoped to get more on his way back. At this point, he was unsure if he was himself or Duke was toying with him. A false sense of control could be devastating after all. He did not feel guilty and sick with fear though. It was almost like Duke had taken the negative emotions he should have felt away with him. That worried him.

Earl worked at the Bureau of Motor Vehicles as a Motor Vehicle License Examiner. His job required him to talk to people, conduct road tests, evaluate driver performance, and inspect driving schools. He also made sure that only qualified persons were provided with driving licenses.

His job required Earl to be charismatic and able to pay attention to details, which was something Duke was better at. He also got to be with people alone—a lot. Earl gulped at the thought, and he was having far too many unnecessary thoughts.

"Is there a point fighting it?"

"Leave me alone. I don't want to talk to you," he grumbled as he took out his phone. Earl remembered that he had missed a call from Mr. Johnson. He respected the man even if he did not agree with the way he did things or the way he had wanted things to be done.

"I'll call him back later." He said to himself, and he probably wouldn't, and he thought and scowled. If he could stall his inevitable scolding, then he would. He dressed up and left the apartment, locking the door behind him. He had this elaborate ritual for locking the door.

He would turn the lock three times to the left another three times to the right and once to the left again. ***"Why do you do that?"***

"You're awfully chatty today," Earl grumbled, and Duke laughed.

THE CREST HILL DINER HAD BEEN THERE FOREVER AND remained a popular spot for most of the town folks. It doubled as a coffeehouse too. Earl had been coming to have breakfast here for the past four years since he had moved to the main town from Mr. Johnson's ranch. Earl especially liked Big Joe's pancakes and would order a cappuccino to go after he had gotten his breakfast.

Big Joe, who ran the diner, always gave him an extra helping of flapjacks and used to joke that if Earl stopped coming to his diner, he would run out of business.

"Hey, Big Joe! Can I have my usual?" He said aloud. He was trying his very best to be as cheerful as he usually was.

Earl sat in his usual chair and waited for Big Joe to come out front. A little while later, someone came out of the back through the small doors that led from the kitchens.

Earl raised his head, a smile on his face, thinking Big Joe was coming out with his food.

"Final..." His voice trailed away, and he froze. The person he was seeing looked nothing like Big Joe. Earl could feel his breath hitch in his chest. The woman who came out was petite and breathtakingly beautiful. She had brown eyes and looked like she was not an inch taller than five'6. Her black hair had streaks of blonde in it and Earl was captivated. She reminded him of his mother, and he felt embarrassed when he realized he was staring.

The most captivating thing about her was her smile. When she smiled, her white teeth stood out against her tanned skin and her brown eyes sparkled, giving her a look of life.

For a full minute, Earl could not utter a word. He did not realize that he had stood to his feet and that his mouth was wide open. It finally registered in his head, and he sat back down with an awkward laugh.

Phew…

She smiled at him; luckily she did not consider what he just did as weird, or rather she was too polite to point it out. His eyes went from the top of her head, almost like he was memorizing her facial features. Her almond-shaped eyes and pert nose. And those lips…His eyes lingered on her lips. They looked like they could make a man go crazy.

"Umm… hi. What can I get you?" She asked, looking at him with a quizzical look. Earl looked down at her name tag.

Ciara… beautiful name to go with a beautiful face.

Earl cleared his throat, his face going red. He did not have time to be too embarrassed as she smiled again, making him feel at ease. He quickly composed himself and smiled back at her.

"Umm… I am sorry. It is just that I was expecting to see Big Joe. You are definitely not Big Joe." He said lamely. She laughed, a soft, tinkling sound that filled the air. Her laughter made Earl think about how sweet honey would feel sliding down one's throat.

"No, I am not Big Joe. My name is Ciara." She said, gesturing to her name tag, "Big Joe is out of town and will be for a while. He had a family emergency to take care of the back home." Ciara explained further.

Earl was not listening. His eyes had fallen on her lips again and he had lost his train of thought. Her lips were small, full, and seemed to be curved in a perpetual smile. Were they as sweet to taste as they looked? Earl thought.

"Snap out of it! You will make her think you are a creep." Came Duke's voice in his head bringing Earl back to the present. Duke was right. Ciara was already beginning to look at him funny.

"Alright then. I will make sure to call him. Do you have his cell number?" Earl said and she nodded. She gestured to the plaque above the bar on where Big Joe had scribbled his cell number. Earl nodded.

"So, what would you have?" She asked him, taking out her notepad from her apron, ready to take his order.

"I will be having my usual." He said without thinking. He was still reeling from how he felt around this woman he had never met.

She looked at him and raised her eyebrow as if to ask him, "Really?"

Earl chuckled and apologized.

"I will have some pancakes and syrup. Scratch that, a lot of syrup." He told her.

"I see we have someone with a sweet tooth." She said as she scribbled on her notepad, causing Earl to chuckle again. "What drink do you prefer?" She asked without looking up from her notepad.

"I will have the orange juice. Then a cappuccino to go." He said and she wrote that down quickly.

"I will be right back with your order." She said and turned away. Earl got a good look at her as she walked away. It was all he could do to hold back the whistle.

"Damn, she's hot!" Came Duke's voice.

"Shut up, Duke. We don't talk about women like that. Be respectful." Earl whispered, placing his elbows on the counter and using his hands to shield his mouth. Other people were in the diner, and he wanted to avoid funny looks.

"Respect my ass. You were already behaving like a lovesick puppy. Staring at her like a wimp. You were not thinking respectful thoughts just now." Duke retorted.

"No, I was not!" Earl said and Duke just laughed. Ciara was back with his breakfast before he could say anything more to Duke.

"Thank you," Earl said when she served him. She smiled and walked towards another customer, a regular just like him.

"Thank you." Duke mimicked in a singsong voice. Earl ignored him and dug into his breakfast. He finished his food and paid, leaving a generous tip for Ciara. He walked out of the diner with his cappuccino.

He was definitely coming back.

GETTING TO THE BUREAU OF MOTOR VEHICLES, HE WENT directly to his superior's office. Earl had already prepared the story to tell him.

Jim Harris had been his boss for the four years Earl had been working at the BMV. Earl had won the Employee of the Month award for three consecutive months and was sure Jim would cut him some slack.

"Earl! Where have you been? You did not come to work yesterday and did not call. You did not pick up my calls either." The older man said, a look of compassion on his face.

"Uh…Mr. Harris. I am sorry. I was not feeling too well." Earl explained. "I may have caught a stomach bug and had to visit the hospital yesterday. I apologize that I did not call you or pick up your calls."

"Oh, Earl. You could have informed me." Jim answered. "You still look like you are not feeling too well. Let me know if you need some more days off. God knows you have earned them."

"That will not be necessary. I am feeling much better now. Thank you, Mr. Harris." Earl replied and walked out of his supervisor's office. He ran into Bertha, his co-worker.

"Earl! Where have you been? I was going to come by your apartment today if you did not turn up again." She said, hugging him. He had helped watch her children a few times. The demon children did not know how to behave but Earl pretended to like them.

"Hi, Bertha. I was not feeling too well yesterday." He replied. Bertha looked at him closely and nodded. "I am alright now though and back to work." He explained, flexing his arms and smiling at her.

"I knew something was wrong. I told Kyle that you would not just miss work. I will bring soup by for you this evening after work." She said, patting him on the shoulder, smiling tenderly at him. Earl nodded and proceeded to his desk.

Kyle Jenkins walked into the office with his normal swagger. Kyle and Earl had gone to high school together; needless to say, he was a pain in the ass.

"Well, if it isn't Earl, the runaway employee of the month," Kyle said, the animosity evident in his voice. "Bertha said you were not feeling too well. I hope it is nothing contagious? You probably should have stayed home for another day just to be sure."

Kyle was a bully and had always been right from high school. He hated the fact that Earl was doing better than him and was liked by everyone.

"It is probably time to take care of him too. But he would be a bonus, not the main act." Duke said, his voice laced with anger. Earl shook his head, trying to silence Duke. Not here. He could not be thinking those thoughts here.

"I am fine; thank you for asking, Kyle." He said instead and continued to look through some license registration papers he had yet to process.

Kyle stomped off, seeing that Earl did not take the bait. Bertha came back into the office and took her seat beside Earl.

"Have you seen the news today? They said a young high school student found a dead woman close to the high school. I heard it was a gruesome sight." She said, shaking her head. Earl slowly raised his head, trying his best not to show any reactions.

"What dead woman?" He asked innocently.

"Finally, someone will appreciate what we've done. The news is spreading fast. I can already smell the fear in the atmosphere."

He grimaced

"Some sick bastard killed a woman and dumped her body in front of the high school," Bertha said. "It is all over the news."

"Sick bastard?! How dare she call us a sick bastard?"

"Shut up…" Earl growled, slamming his fist into a wall and startling her. "That's horrible; how could anyone do such a thing?"

Bertha frowned; she felt sorry for Earl as he palmed his face. She imagined that the news must have been too heavy for a man of his nature. ***"I never knew you were an actor…."*** Duke teased as his breathing became labored and he managed to escape the conversation. He quickly got up, overturning his chair.

"I'm sorry, Bertha." He said, "I need a moment,"

"No…. it's fine. I'm sorry," She apologized as he rushed off towards the men's room.

"Are you alright, Earl? Your stomach still bothering you?" a colleague called after him, but he did not answer.

Earl did not turn his back until he was sure he was alone. He got into a stall and locked it.

"How dare she? We did them a favor and this is how they would thank us?" Duke ranted.

Earl worked on calming down. He tried to ignore Duke.

"No one understands us or our assignment."

"Fucking shut up! There's no bloody assignment. You're just insane."

"Insane…" Duke repeated but then began to laugh. Earl walked out of the stall and washed his face at the sink. His hands were shaking.

"Pull yourself together, Duke." He admonished himself. He could not call unwanted attention to himself. "You're going to screw us over at this rate."

He turned to leave but then his legs would not obey him; he was suddenly lightheaded and could do nothing but stare into the mirror where his reflection glared back at him.

"Need I remind you…" Duke started as he reached into his mouth and pulled a tooth out. Earl's eyes screamed in pain, but his body stood there staring at the bloody tooth in his hand. **"I'm doing this for us… we are in this together and you know it."**

"I don't want this…"

"Don't cry now… you were cursing a moment ago. You never fucking curse, and that's my thing but I'll allow it. Now that we're finally coexisting as equals."

"You're a fucking monster; I'm nothing like you!" Earl snapped, tossing his tooth aside and turning what was once pain to rage for Duke within him.

"You're right... you're not a monster. Not yet." Duke laughed as Earl's rage died into to fear at the sight of how twisted a smile his own face could make. ***"You didn't take your meds... you thought I wouldn't notice?"***

"They were bad-"

"Then why aren't you counting. If you wanted me gone... I'd be gone," Duke smirked as Earl stroked his chin. ***"It's fine. I need you just as you need me... together we'll be."***

"Jesus Christ!" Kyle gasped as he stepped in and saw Earl over the sink, "Are you okay?"

"My bad... I got a little lightheaded and well- you can see how it ended." Earl explained with a frown and a groan as Kyle rushed over to him with a napkin. "It's fine. Nothing a little ice can't fix."

"Geez... first the stomachache now this?!" Kyle scowled, "It's almost like your luck's gone to shit."

"You're right. We should fix that" Earl chuckled as he washed his face and turned to leave.

"You okay?"

"Yeah... ***We're fine,***" They answered with a smirk as they left.

CHAPTER
THREE

Today was not one of the good days. Sure, it was sunny with the birds in the sky and everything, but it was still as shitty as any day could get. Detective Anita Heath alighted from her old car and slammed its door shut behind herself. She was already in a bad mood. She had barely woken up when she received the call about this murder.

What a way to start the day, she thought bitterly.

To make things worse, her five-year-old daughter had thrown a fit that morning as she drove her to the daycare and Anita was in no mood to deal with anyone. All before she had managed to get her morning coffee. She walked over to the crime scene. The area had been cordoned off with the yellow crime scene investigation tape.

The naked body was propped on a tree beside the school's side entrance—the sick bastard.

She ducked under the tape and approached the body after flashing her badge to the policeman who had been stationed to watch who went in and came out.

Detective Pete Morales, her partner stood over the dead body, a look of horror on his face. He was a rookie who had just graduated from the Police Academy. From the look of things, it was his first time seeing something like this.

"Good morning, Detective Heath." Pete greeted, his face white as a sheet. She looked at his face and felt pity for him. Even after years of being in the police force, Anita had never gotten used to seeing things like this.

"Good morning, Pete. Why don't you go across the street and get me some coffee?" She asked him, allowing him to take a walk and clear his head. Not that this image would ever leave him. The first crime scene would always remain with you.

Pete looked at her gratefully and walked away from the body, ducking under the crime scene tape. He could not get out of there fast enough.

Other cops from the precinct were trying to keep the crowd of onlookers, mostly school students back and asking questions.

They had covered the body with a sheet and the crime scene investigators were looking around. Anita crouched beside it, bracing herself. She lifted the edge of the sheet closer to her and looked underneath. The sight that greeted her eyes made her stomach heave. She was thankful that she had not gotten round to eating anything yet.

The first thing that hit her was the look of horror on the woman's face. She must have suffered before she had died. Across her forehead, the killer had carved out the number seven with a sharp object. The sick bastard had even made her up. The lipstick on her lips looked fresh. The girl's hands were tied behind her back and her arms looked raw.

He must have tied her to a pole or something. The lack of blood and the fact that her arms looked like they had been tied to something let Anita know that she had not been killed at this spot. It was only the dump site.

A very public and strategic dump site. This killer knew exactly what he was doing dumping her here. He had even posed her. This place must be symbolic to the killer, she thought. She looked carefully around the body and noticed drag marks.

Anita looked closer at the woman's folded hands. No doubt, he had posed her after killing her. What caught her attention was a small piece of paper between the woman's fingers.

"May I have some tweezers?" Anita asked. The woman nodded and rummaged in her kit for one. She handed a small tweezer to Anita who used it to pry the piece of paper from the dead woman's fingers. The paper was folded up. Using her gloved hands, Anita spread the piece of paper.

The words:

***HERE LAY THE SECOND* - SOPHIA MYERS - THE PRIDEFUL SLUT.**

SHE DESERVED TO DIE. ANOTHER EVIL OUT OF THE WORLD. WRATH WAS FIRST

were written in bold letters with a marker. The handwriting was neat, lovely penmanship she could add.

Anita was taken aback. Was not every day she got a letter from a mysterious killer. The handwriting was almost artistic with a fine degree to its calligraphy. If only solving the case would have been as easy as getting a note from every suspect in town, but sadly they had none yet.

She sighed and asked the technician for a zip lock bag so they could carefully place the note inside it while wondering what it meant. She looked at the body again and the way it was positioned. Most people would see a body, but she saw an even bolder message; it was as if the killer had wanted to shame her, even in death.

A grudge maybe?

Who would do such a sick thing? What did the number seven mean? And what did he mean by '… Wrath was first?'

Anita let the sheet fall back on the body. She had seen enough.

"Hey there!" She called the crime scene technician closest to her. The man turned and walked towards her.

"Has anyone tried to find the murder site? This is not where she was killed." She asked. The man looked confused and scratched his head. Anita was annoyed; she thought that much was obvious.

Who the heck sent a rookie to a crime scene? She turned on her heels, barely keeping herself from spitting with annoyance. If you want to see something done, you would have to do it yourself.

She carefully followed the trail. Her hunger and need for caffeine were all but forgotten. Walking further, she noticed the drag marks becoming deeper. She followed the trail deeper into the grove of trees, towards the small lake. It was ironic that the guy would choose this particular grove of trees seeing that there was a legend about a woman found dead in the woods.

The sick bastard has a twisted sense of humor. That or there was another reason why he had chosen this place. Anita continued to follow the drag marks, carefully watching her steps to avoid destroying any evidence the killer might have left. The trail ended at a large oak tree.

Anita saw blood around the base of the tree, most likely from the head wounds and what looked like new ropes tied around the tree. No sign of the woman's clothes. She looked around the tree and the surrounding area, looking for anything she could use. This guy was meticulous too.

She drew out her radio and called for a crime scene tech.

"I have found the murder site. Send the team." She described the small path she had taken to them before dropping the radio back into her pocket. When the crime scene guys arrived, Anita followed the trail back to where the body was.

"Where is the kid who found the body?" She asked Pete who had returned with her coffee. She showed Pete the note as she took a deep sip and sighed, closing her eyes. She had needed that. Pete pointed at one of the squad cars parked along the street.

"What does this note mean by 'Another'? Has there been a murder we did not know about?" Pete asked Anita.

"Not that I know of. They are either playing with us or referring to something or someplace we are unaware of. That is what we need to find out. We will look at old case files to see if there is any that matches this murder." She informed Pete.

"Have you talked to him?" Anita asked, gesturing to the boy who had found the body.

"No, ma'am. He was too shocked to talk. The only thing he did was call 911 and the operator had said he could barely speak." Pete answered.

"Poor kid." She said and turned towards the car. She hoped he had been able to pull himself together by now. He was in the middle of this mess, whether he liked it or not. Pete walked behind her as they approached the car.

"What's his name?" She asked just before they got to the car.

"Jon Reyes," Pete informed her. She nodded. The boy was a redheaded, squinty-eyed teen who looked to be on the bad side of puberty. His face was riddled with acne and his mess of ginger hair made him look like a hobo. His eyes were a faded blue which Anita was sure was made even duller by the shock and fright the boy must have experienced.

"Hey, Jon. How are you doing?" She asked. She could see him shaking in fright. She felt pity for him, subconsciously thanking God her daughter had been spared the ordeal. She had seen a fair share of death and human cruelty, and it usually took her weeks to get over seeing such things completely. The things human beings were capable of doing to other human beings.

She shook her head, trying to clear it. She needed to be at the top of her game and could not let emotions cloud her judgment. At least not now.

She had thought moving to a small town would spare her these kinds of cases. After eleven years of being a detective in New York, she had sought transfer to a small town, tired of the Big Apple and its onslaught of gruesome and mostly senseless crimes. After her husband had died, she had thought it would be best to bring her daughter to the relatively quiet town of Crest Hill, where she had grown up and lived life at a much quieter pace.

She remembered her husband fondly, thinking how she was the woman she was because of him. He had been a police officer too and had been killed in the line of duty. Steve had been a very good man, husband, and father. He had helped her forget the pain and anguish she had endured in her childhood. Best of all, he had taken his job as a policeman seriously, making sure to do it with integrity.

Apart from being her husband, Steve had been her role model.

Until this morning, her only worry had been about her daughter. Now, this. Out of the blue. She had not seen this coming. Her tiny bubble of paradise had just been shattered.

"I thought I had escaped seeing things like this." She muttered under her breath as she watched the boy rouse himself enough to look at her.

"She is dead right?" Jon Reyes asked as if just waking up.

Anita nodded and watched as the boy crumpled in tears. Poor thing.

"Hey, Jon. You need to do me a favor here. You are the only clue we have, and I want you to pull yourself together and tell me all that you remember." She said, softening her voice and using the tone she would use to coerce her five-year-old to eat her vegetables. The boy sniffed and looked up again.

"I did not see anything. I just came to school, and I saw her lying there naked. I thought it was a mannequin and that someone was playing a sick joke. I even... touched it." Jon said, wringing his hands together. He began to sob then, and Anita knew she was not going to be able to get much out of him anymore. Not now.

"Alright, Jon. You have been of great help. You are a brave young man. When you remember anything else, I will be here." She said and gestured for Pete to follow her.

"Where are his parents?" She asked when they were just out of Jon's earshot.

"His mother is a nurse at the local hospital. She was on the night shift, so we had to call her at the hospital.

She would be here shortly." Pete explained. Anita nodded.

"Anything from passersby or onlookers?" She asked Pete.

"The police have interviewed A few people. Most of them saw and heard nothing." Pete said.

"Gather all the intel you can and meet me back at the precinct in thirty minutes. We have to hit the ground running on this one. This is the first of its kind and it cannot go unsolved. Not on my watch." Anita told Pete with passion.

"Make sure the kid gets the treatment he needs. He would probably need months of therapy. Also, we still need to talk to him so we can go to the house later on with the mother's permission.

"Please, set up a hotline so anyone with clues can call in or let them know they can just walk into the precinct and ask to speak with me." She finished. Pete nodded and walked back toward the crime scene.

Anita went into her car and drove down to the precinct.

"THE WOMAN WHO WAS KILLED HAS FINALLY BEEN identified." Kyle walked into Earl's office with a long face. Bertha looked up from the papers she had been looking through.

"Who is she? Is she someone we know?" She asked, standing up from her seat and approaching Kyle.

"Yeah. I know her. Earl, you should know her too. It's Sophia Myers." Kyle said, looking at Earl directly in the face. Earl looked up, stupefied.

"Sophia… Myers…?" He asked quizzically. "Nah… you're joking."

"I wish I was"

"Who was she?" Bertha probed as Earl sank back into his chair deflated.

"She was the most beautiful girl in high school and Earl here had a major crush on her." He said, looking from Earl to Bertha. Earl was quiet; the sadness on his face was almost depressing.

"It's been ten years since we left High school, Kyle. I never knew she was back… now she's-" he said, trying to reason with Kyle

Kyle made a sound of disbelief and turned to Bertha.

"I can't believe this happened to someone we knew. Damn..what a horrible way to go." Kyle told Bertha.

"God rest her soul," Bertha said, making the cross sign.

"Such a pity. I like her, but I got over her quickly after that day; I heard she left town immediately after high school. What was she doing back? How unlucky does a person have to be to return only to be killed." Earl continued grimly. He paled so much you would have thought he was close to her. The three of them all got depressed over the gruesome news.

"You're really good at this!" Duke ***laughed*** in his head. ***"But cool it off. We can never be too careful, or you'd give us away."***

"What happened?" Bertha asked.

"Earl here practically proposed to her. Chocolate and flowers and everything but she rejected him, in front of the whole school even." Kyle blurted out.

"Oh…poor Earl. Still embarrassed about what happened ten years ago. Don't worry. It was her loss." Bertha said but caught her breath seeming to realize that the person in question was dead. She made the cross sign again and slowly sat in her chair. "Who would do such a despicable thing?" She asked, leaning her head back on the seat.

"I heard she was in town to see her mother for a bit. She had just gone through a divorce too. Poor thing. Everything seemed to turn against her." Kyle said, shaking his head. He remembered how they all thought she had it all. Now she was not even alive. Her death was even an undignified one. He shook his head and shuddered again.

"The police have asked anyone with information to call their hotline or drop by the precinct." He said, walking out of Earl's office back to his own.

"This is the opportunity we have been waiting for. You need to go to the police station."

Earl stood up immediately and went to the restroom.

"Poor Earl. His stomach is still bothering him. He knocked a thought out. And now his crush has up and been murdered." He heard Bertha say to no one in particular as he walked away.

Earl was sad but still felt like bursting into laughter and barely held it in till he got into the men's room.

"You're a bad influence, Duke," He whispered once he was alone, "And what's this with the station?"

"Trust me. I'll fill you in along the way; everything had gone just as planned. Now for the next phase."

EARL WALKED INTO THE PRECINCT WITH SO MUCH confidence, albeit he had expressed sadness. He looked nothing like himself. He had blond hair now and wore glasses which made him look a good ten years older than he actually was.

"Good afternoon." He greeted the policeman at the front desk. The man was fat and had been nodding off when Earl walked in. The man jerked awake and quickly sat up, rubbing his eyes with the back of his hand.

Was this lazy fuck those who wanted to catch him? He thought, barely hiding his contempt for the man.

"Good afternoon, sir. How may we help you?" The policeman asked, sitting even straighter.

"I am here to report a missing wallet. I was walking on the street when someone bumped into me yesterday afternoon. He must have picked up my pocket, and I did not notice it until I got home."

"What'd he look Like?" the officer asked,

"I did not get a good look at his face. He was wearing a black hoodie and jeans and a cap." He explained to the man who was looking uninterested in what Earl was saying.

The policeman stood up from his chair, reached into the drawer, brought out a legal pad along with a form, and handed it to him.

"Fill out this form and write a statement describing everything in your wallet. You can describe the person you believe picked your pocket if you recollect what he looked like." He then sat back down in his seat again.

Earl scratched his fake moustache trying to look like he was deep in thought. He hid his brown eyes behind a set of blue contacts and glasses. He was having a good laugh inside at these people.

Earl began to fill out the form and write out his statement then paused as if he was thinking.

"It is such a pity about the murdered young lady," Earl said to the man innocently.

"Uhm... I know right. She was one of the most popular kids when she was in high school about ten years ago. I knew her then. Who would have thought she would end up murdered?" The man said sitting up in his chair.

"Have the police uncovered anything on the murderer?" Earl asked innocently. The man shook his head vigorously.

"We have received some calls many of them from people who are jobless and bored. Nothing solid has come up yet."

They can't find anything. We are cleverer than all of these empty heads put together.

Suddenly, the policeman scrambled to his feet.

"Welcome back Detective Heath. Pete." He said, slightly bowing his head. Earl turned his head slightly, careful not to be in full view of whomever the man was greeting. A woman had just walked in. She looked to be in her early thirties but carried herself with so much strength like someone who was younger. She was in plainclothes, but Earl knew she had some authority to her from the way they all scrambled about to attend to her. She had this worldly look about her and her eyes were intelligent like she could see right through anyone.

She looked very serious, and her mouth looked like it was in a frown, like she had seen a fair share of sad things that had made her perpetually sad. There was something about her that commanded his respect though. He refused to examine the feeling. Deep down, the reaction was almost instinctive.

"Is the Chief in, Perry?" She asked, directing her question to the cop behind the counter. The young man who had walked in with her looked like he was new. His face was white, which made his dark hair stand out. His blue eyes looked glazed over and Earl could guess where they must have been coming from.

They must have just come from seeing his work. Earl tried his best not to grin. That would raise suspicions, which he did not need.

Perry shook his head, moving some sheaves of papers around, reading a few unintelligible scribbles he had put down.

"No luck yet Detective. I have been on the phone all day but no one with any real information has called or come in." He said, turning his full attention to the woman and the police officer, whom he assumed was the woman's partner.

Earl was going to slip out when the woman turned and faced him quietly.

"What is your name, sir?" She asked him.

"Duke. Duke Harris." He replied with a smile, trying to sound like James Bond. "You do good work here. Well done." He said, giving her a thumbs up. Then he walked out of the police station.

Duke chuckled as he left but yet Earl could not shake his unease.

"They definitely are no match for us."

DETECTIVE HEATH STOOD LOOKING AFTER THE MAN THAT had walked out of the precinct. He had given them a compliment but why did she feel like he was making fun of them? The guy gave her the creeps and her gut was telling her something was wrong. He looked funny and unnatural, making her think he had been wearing a disguise. It was either that or she was finally feeling the effects of ingesting caffeine on an empty stomach. She was a paranoid woman, but her paranoia made her so damn good at her job.

"What did that gentleman want?" She asked Perry.

"Oh. He came in to report a missing wallet. He said someone picked his pocket." Perry replied. Anita approached his desk and picked up the legal pad with the man's statement. The handwriting was neat but hurried and the statement was meticulously written.

He had described the man who had bumped into him with so many details. Black cap, black hoodie, and jeans. Something did not feel right.

She shook the feeling off and walked into the Chief's office. He was a big African American man who she had grown to respect for his work ethics and care for his team. The man raised his head when Anita and Pete walked into his office.

"Detective Heath. Officer Morales." He acknowledged their presence and gestured them into the small seats opposite him.

"Ann, what do you think we should do now?" The Chief asked. He was the only person who ever got away with calling her "Ann" at the precinct. She absolutely hated being called that.

The Chief had already received the reports from the crime scene people and was aware that the hotlines had received more prank calls than any useful information.

"Chief, this particular crime does not look like it would be the last one. There is going to be more. Unfortunately, that may be our only chance of ever catching him, unless the crime tech people can miraculously find a definitive clue on her." She said, tapping her finger on the edge of the desk.

Anita had seen her fair share of such crimes. The precision with which this murderer had worked pointed towards a demented mind. The amount of time and patience it must have taken him to carve the number seven on her forehead spoke of someone with a bizarre and sick mind.

Chief Doyle sighed and slumped in his chair. He looked tired and suddenly like he had aged ten years since yesterday. The big man looked like he was going to have a breakdown. Anita was sure he was under pressure to get this murderer. For a small town that has never experienced this kind of crime before, Anita knew it could be overwhelming.

"In my thirty-five years of being in the police force, I have never seen something as gory and evil as this." He said in a whisper, rifling through the crime scene photos that had been brought to him. He shook his head and closed the folder, shoving it into a drawer.

Anita could only nod. The Chief's career had always been in small towns where the police's only problems were rambunctious teenagers who were getting drunk and vandalizing public properties on the weekend. She on the other hand, had seen a lot. Too much in fact.

"What else have the crime scene people found out?" Chief Doyle asked. She shook her head.

"Nothing, Chief. The guy was meticulous. He left no trace of himself behind. The ropes he used were new and he took all of the woman's clothes away with him. There was no sign of sexual intercourse, so no seminal fluid or any other bodily fluids. We could not find any hairs either except the girl's hair." Anita explained.

"How about the object he used to disfigure her face? Any clue on it?" The Chief asked.

"None. Except that it was stainless steel and was most likely an object with a flat mouth, like a chisel. He did not leave it behind either." Anita explained.

The chief sighed, looking more tired.

"The mother of the deceased? Has anyone been to her place?" He then asked.

"Pete and I planned on going there immediately after reporting to you." She told the chief, who nodded and looked at Pete.

"How are you holding up, officer Morales?" Knowing he was new; Chief Doyle could only imagine how shocking it must have been.

"I am doing fine Chief. It was a shock at first, though. Thank you for asking." Pete replied, as polite as ever.

"The kid who found the body... have you been able to talk with him?" Chief Doyle asked, turning his attention again to Anita.

"His mother was afraid for his mental health and asked us to postpone his questioning by a day. I will be going over to their house tomorrow to talk with him. He was shocked and could not answer my questions earlier when we met." Anita explained.

"I can only imagine. Poor child. He will be scarred for life. Ann!" A note of urgency crept into the chief's voice when he called her name.

"Yes, sir!"

"We need to find this bastard. We cannot let someone like that keep roaming the streets." He said, leaning back in his chair, clearly exhausted.

"Find out why the number seven. That may be our first step. Then, why the school?" He said, dismissing Anita.

She walked out of the Chief's office and towards the reception on their way out.

"Any helpful information?" She asked.

They were on their way to the victim's mother's house. She lived in an apartment building on Weeping Willow Street, not so far from the High School with her mother. They would talk with the mother.

"Nothing new from the crime scene. The medical examiner has examined the corpse, although yet to perform the autopsy. He noticed that the carving on her forehead and her bruises were done while she was still alive." Pete said.

Anita took a sharp breath and turned to look at Pete, who had the same look of horror she had on her own face. That was very sick. But it did say something about the killer.

"He wanted to inflict as much pain as possible. Very likely a crime of passion. She knew her killer. I noticed that the lipstick was fresh. He probably put it on her. The medical examiner would confirm that." Anita declared without breaking her stride. They got into her car and Pete drove.

"Why do you think so? Besides, nothing points towards the gender of the killer yet." He said, trying to follow Anita's logic.

"Well, you would only take your time to inflict so much pain on someone you know. The killer probably thinks the victim deserved that amount of pain for something she had done to them. And you are right; the killer could also be female. They may have been jealous of the victim's beauty or something around it, hence the lipstick." Anita said. Learning something about the killer opened more doors to questions.

"One thing I know is that this cannot be the only thing this person has done. There must be precedents. Also, check the area around the victim's house. I believe she may have met her killer there. Also, add my cell number to the hotlines. I do not trust that cop at the reception. I have caught him sleeping on duty a lot of times." She answered. Pete nodded and continued to drive.

The victim's house was on the other side of town, a much quieter place than where the precinct was situated. Anita looked around the place, trying to see how a person could just go missing without being seen. The streets were quiet, most likely because of what had happened, but she could say it was this way on a normal day.

There was a block of commercial stores across from the apartment building. The grove where she had been found was about two blocks away, a mere five-to-ten-minute walk from her apartment building.

Anita and Pete walked into the apartment building and took the stairs to the third floor. They knocked on the door of Apartment 3D and waited. At first, there was no sound, and then someone opened the door a little.

"Who is it?" An old voice asked through the crack.

"It's the police ma'am. We are here to ask a few questions about your daughter." Anita said, looking at Pete.

"Hasn't she been notified about her daughter's death?" Anita mouthed so that only Pete could hear her.

"She has." He said and nodded.

It was a bit strange how the woman was acting. One would think she'd have family members around to begin preparing for the funeral or at least ask questions. The door was opened wider, allowing Anita and Pete to squeeze through. The whole house was a mess. There was clutter everywhere and the house smelled like an incense factory

"Hello, Miss. Hernandez." Anita greeted the disheveled woman standing in front of her. The woman's wild mess of black and grey hair stood out in different directions. Her eyes looked dull, and her hands would just jerk all on their own.

This woman should not be living by herself, Anita thought. The living room, if it could be called was dusty and full of clutter, and it looked like at least ten years of clutter.

"Well, come in." She said, leading them deeper into the room and gesturing for them to sit on some straight-backed chairs. She herself sat down on a beanbag she had set up directly opposite them.

"First of all, Miss. Hernandez, we are so sorry for your loss. We apologize for coming in to disturb your grieving but the circumstances surrounding your daughter's death warrants this." She spoke.

The woman just nodded, saying nothing. She looked like she was not in this world at all. Anita noticed some bottles of whiskey and wondered if she was drunk. She would not blame her though. Losing one's only child in such a way could drive someone into drunkenness.

"We just have a few questions. You can answer us as honestly as you can." Pete said while the woman nodded.

"When was the last time you saw Sophia, ma'am?" Pete asked, taking out his notepad and pen.

"She was home with me all day that day. I remember that she did not want to get out of bed the whole day but finally did when she ran out of cigarettes. We had an argument. She does not like the smells of my incense and I asked her to get out if she did not like them. I pray to my gods with them." The woman sniffed and tears rolled down her cheek. Anita handed her a tissue she had brought for that exact purpose. The woman took it and wiped her face with it.

"So that was the last time you saw her. How was she mentally during her stay with you?" Pete asked. The woman nodded.

"She stomped out saying she wanted to buy cigarettes." Miss. Hernandez told them.

"She had just been through a divorce and came home to regroup before going back to start her life afresh. My Sophia was one of the most popular girls in high school, but she left town immediately after that for college. Her father and I split just around that time. She had not been home in ten years, and I was overjoyed that my daughter was back with me albeit under those circumstances. I felt responsible to some extent for having set a precedent. She just wanted to find her bearings and get back on her feet..." The woman continued but her voice trailed off as she made the last statement.

The pain and anguish Anita could see in the woman's face and hear in her voice caused her to grit her teeth. Her own daughter was still quite young, and she could not imagine losing her to some crazy person's evil mind. Young or old, people's children remain just that to them...children.

"Please find who did this to my Sophia." The woman said, slipping off of the bean bag into the floor on her knees. Her sobs came then, wracking her whole little frame. Anita held unto the woman helping her to her feet. She smelt of mold and incense. Anita wondered the last time Miss. Hernandez had ever ventured out of her house.

"We will do our best, ma'am. Be strong. For Sophia. Call me if anything comes up at all." Anita said, handing the woman her card. They sat together with her hearing stories of the deceased while she had been young before finally taking their leave a while later.

"This is so heartbreaking. Can we contact the family to come to see this woman? I fear for her health both mental and physical." Pete said. Miss. Hernandez had told them that all her family was no longer in town and her ex-husband was in Europe with his wife.

"You do that," Anita replied. Just then, a call came in. She picked up her cell phone and looked at the screen. It was an unknown number.

"Hello," Anita said, picking up the call and placing the phone to her ear.

"Hello, Detective Heath. I have information about the murderer."

CHAPTER
FOUR

It was all he could do to not chuckle as he heard the detective's voice when she picked up his call.

"I have information about the murderer," Earl said in Duke's raspy voice. He smiled at his reflection in the mirror, admiring himself.

"Oh, alright. I appreciate your call. What is your name, sir? And what can you tell us about them?" She asked.

"Oh, my name is Henry Johnson." Using the name of one of Mr. Johnson's children.

"I was around the woman's apartment building at about 6 PM. I saw the place on the news and thought, wow, I was just there and around the same time she had been there. It could have been me." Earl said while Duke was making surprised faces in the mirror.

"Then when I saw her picture on the news I was like, I saw this woman on that day. I went into the grocery store to buy some toiletry and a six-pack of beer when she entered the grocery store. I remember thinking, wow, she is beautiful, you know?

"Not long after she had walked into the grocery store, some man walked in after her. I did not see his face, but he had a black hoodie on with a black cap that obscured his face. His clothes were all black too. I did not pay him much attention except to think, and this guy must be strong because he looked like a bodybuilder to me." Earl dictated grimly but quickly.

"What was the most baffling was that he did not buy anything but followed her when she left the store after buying her pack of cigarettes. I promptly forgot about her and the man until I saw the news." Earl finished.

"Oh...can you come to the station to put down your statement?" The detective asked

"Sure. I can come in first thing in the morning." He replied. "I hope I have been of utmost help. I wouldn't want to have wasted your time detective. I keep thinking, what if I had walked up to her? Maybe she would still be alive."

"Oh no. You have been the most helpful. Thank you for calling and we would expect to see you tomorrow." She said and hung up.

Duke burst into full laughter, But Earl sat there for a moment. ***"All according to plan. Just like I said"***

"This feels too easy. She sounded… off." Earl shrugged it off, "Forget it. I'm hungry."

He concluded and then went down to the diner for dinner.

"I THINK WE HAVE JUST CAUGHT A BREAK. OUR KILLER just gave us a call." Anita told Pete with a sigh. Pete was visibly confused; he had been scribbling everything the man had said. What was all this about the killer calling all of a sudden?

"Huh? How could you be so sure?" He finally asked.

"I could hear it in his voice, he sounded convincing enough, but it was way too obvious he was trying to throw us off" She grimaced, "In all my years as a detective, I've found that killers, especially the narcissistic and psychopathic kind would try to inject themselves into the investigation of their victims. He wanted front row seats to his own execution and doing so threw him under the bus."

"You're not making any sense," Pete scowled as she palmed her face. She was monologuing again.

"He just gave information that hasn't been released to the public. We mentioned that she had last been seen going to the grocery store, but no one mentioned what she went to buy. This guy said she went to buy cigarettes." Anita finished. "I was hoping for this, makes catching the freak easier for us."

The light of understanding dawned on Pete's eyes.

"Can we not trace the call?" He asked excitedly, even as he realized that was just wishful thinking.

"We're in the middle of nowhere; we don't have the means. Even if I could get a favor from a friend, I bet it would be a bust." She mused. "It would be a burner cell. Let's cover all our bases, and I can bet every dime of my monthly that no one will be coming to give a statement at the precinct tomorrow." She said and got back into the car. Pete got in too and they returned to the precinct.

All they could do was hope their killer would be egoistic enough to call again or make another mistake.

Before he decided to kill another person.

EARL SAT AT THE COUNTER WATCHING CIARA AS SHE served customers. She moved lithely and with a grace that seemed to come from years of being on her feet. Like a dancer. He had gotten his third refill of coffee and was tempted to get another just so he could get another gander at her lovely smile, and he was sure she would smile. He did not even try to make conversation with her, at the time, he was satisfied with watching her work.

He was glad he had brought his little camera with him. It still had Sophia's pictures on it but that did not stop him from surreptitiously taking photos of her. It did not really matter that she was not in a pose, photo of her was satisfactory. He was going to find a way of developing the photos he took; Earl was always a fan of having something tangible that he could hold on to.

Ciara loved her job and it showed. Every time she turned to him. Her smile made his insides turn jelly, and he could feel himself melt into a puddle.

"You're being weird again."

"Let me have this…" He sighed into his cup of coffee. "You're still mad. I decided we're not going to the precinct, aren't you?"

"It's fine. At least this one seems worthy."

Worthy or not, she was the only thing on his mind as he stepped out. Earl figured staying in the diner more than he needed would draw unnecessary attention, so he decided to change his pace. He lurked in the shadows again that night, watching from behind a tree as she and her friend locked up. Tonya. Tonya was nothing like her.

Tonya was a tall blonde girl probably a year or two older than Ciara was. She was a loud-mouthed girl who worked at the diner with Ciara. She hardly ever shut up and was always talking up a storm. Neither Earl nor Duke liked her one bit. When they had locked the store up, he followed them. He was careful not to be noticed. Earl had gotten better at tailing people; they could never have seen him shadowing them. They lived together or at least in the same apartment building. It made sense that they walked in together.

Enough for tonight, Earl thought.

He was getting antsy. Too much caffeine. He contemplated just going back home but decided against it. The night was still young, he thought.

Or…

He could do something he had always wanted to do.

Rather than heading home immediately, he took to the streets. It was still a bit early and yet the streets had fallen silent. Deserted and devoid of life's noise save for the night breeze's rustle and crickets. They had done this. They the chosen, had instilled fear in the masses. Everybody was terrified; they had hidden in their little houses too afraid to be outside after dark. What they did not know was that he could get anyone he wanted at any time he wanted. Their doors could not keep him out. He had been chosen for just that.

Funny, the glee in his heart used to be fear until a day ago. He laughed out loud like a deranged person; the moment had this intoxicating delusion of power to it. Earl stood still in the middle of the street. Slowly, a strange feeling of loneliness began to creep into his mind. He could not feel Duke's presence; rather than freedom and power, he felt weak. He was convinced that he wanted this, then why did he feel so wrong?

He walked home, forlorn and ladened with guilt. By the time he reached his apartment, his mind was in shambles. He could not remember the last time he had taken his medications- he had thrown them away after all. He had not been sleeping well either. The sleeping pills had not been working. Deep and excruciating pain started from his chest and spread to his back. He fell to his knees holding his chest. He needed help.

Mr. Johnson came to his mind in his time of need, so he took out his cell phone and called him. He did not care that it was past midnight. He wanted to talk, and he was going to talk.

The man picked up after the third ring and Earl was filled with relief.

"Earl?" The groggy voice said over the phone. He must have been sleeping.

"Mr. Johnson." Earl blubbered, tears and snot dripping down his face.

"What is it, son?" Mr. Johnson asked with so much concern in his voice.

"I… don't know." Earl choked out. He sat on the floor and began to rock himself back and forth.

"Have you been taking your meds, Earl?" The man asked him. Earl stopped rocking, quickly regretting his decision to call the man.

"You idiot… What're you doing!"

Earl froze up. Scared and confused.

"Why did you call him? He and the others always want to keep you bound to those drugs. Never again! Let us be free and live our life."

"I am sorry to bother you, Mr. Johnson." He said in a monotone and hung up. Mr. Johnson was worried, he called back several times, but Earl did not pick up. He could not; Duke did not let him. The only thing he could do was lay there in pain and watch as it rang.

Earl was alone in the world. No one had ever really understood him, and everyone had left him all on his own. First his sister and then his mother. The memories of that time hit him hard at that moment that he began to sob. Deep, wracking sobs shook his body.

The memories of a childhood he wanted to forget clawing at his skull in a migraine.

CHAPTER
FIVE

Only innocence could describe the look in young Earl's eyes. He sat on his branch on the large oak tree in front of their small house. It had become his favorite spot. Not that there was anything special about it. The tree was far enough from the house for him to avoid being beaten but close enough for him to still hear his father's bellows as he landed blows on his mother. This was his escape. Earl could see the entrance to the house from his tree, but no one could see him.

They lived on a large plot of land, far enough from the main town that no one could really hear what was going on at their house. They were isolated and never had any visitors. Their closest neighbor was a good ten-minute walk away from them.

"I hate him so much," Earl said to no one in particular.

"Well, we could kill him." A voice he knew very well said to him. Earl shook his head, trying to dispel the voice but could not. He had begun to hear the voice of a boy his age when he was three years old. At first, the boy only said things that made him happy. The voice cheered him up.

Earl was eleven years old and had no friends except Duke who had grown up with him. This only worsened his friendless state because he and Duke carried on conversations, and since no one else saw Duke, he was seen as a crazy kid. Earl did not mind it at all, and he could not bring any real friends over to his house anyway. At best, the place was a pigsty not to talk of the constant fights and his father's incessant drunkenness. Earl could not remember if he had ever seen his mother's face without any fresh scars, especially in the past five years.

Tom Hughes was a big man given to drinking and huge temper outbursts. Once he was angry, no one or nothing was spared. Earl had found it easier to just not be around the man. His mother, on the other hand, had no choice.

"I cannot kill father," Earl said drawing seven circles in two places on the tree trunk with his sharpie. There was something about the number seven. He found the number both fascinating and frightening. He did not know why but doing things in multiples of seven always soothed him. Right from when he was little, he had to do things in multiples of seven in order for things to make sense.

Earl had not known why he always had the compulsion to repeat everything in multiples of seven and everyone, including his father thought he was crazy. Only his mother never looked at him wrong whenever he had to turn around in circles seven times or if he thumped his head or leg seven times.

Duke told him that the number seven was a symbol of spirituality and that Earl had been chosen. Earl was sure that it always helped him calm down, especially when his father began to yell.

"Yes, we can. You know where he keeps the gun. And no one would miss him anyway. Your mother would be free. Think about it." Duke said. Earl began to be agitated, his breaths came in a sharp burst, and he could barely catch his breath. He jumped down from the branch he had been hiding in.

As he thumped his head on one side with his fist seven times and another seven times on the other side, he felt his heart rate stabilize and his breathing became even. He tapped his forefinger on his thigh seven times and stood still. Duke was silent and Earl could feel himself become calm.

He could still hear his father's voice though.

"Useless woman. Can't do nothing' right." The man slurred as he stumbled out of the house towards his truck. Earl hoped he would be involved in an accident and never return. The pulsing seven on his forehead glowed even brighter. He was drunk enough to cause an accident as it was. He got into the truck and within seconds, Earl's father had driven off, a cloud of dust and a spray of gravel in his wake.

Earl's mother, Rose came out of the house after the vehicle had turned the corner at the road and gone out of sight. She was holding her right side, walking with a limp carrying a pail in her right hand. She was headed towards the well. As usual, her face was swollen and already turning blue.

Earl watched her walk out of the house and contemplated the woman who had birthed him wondering how she could allow herself to keep enduring his mule of a father, especially with her background.

Rose Hughes, formally Dupree, was a petite woman, demure in speech and character. She must have been beautiful before she met his father, Earl thought. When he was younger, she held him in her lap and told him stories of where and how she had grown up. She had been born with a silver spoon and her parents had doted on her.

"Grandma said I was spoilt rotten." She would say while showing him old pictures of her family before she met Tom Hughes. His mother told him that she used to live on a large estate with her parents and two sisters.

She had been the last child and had been given everything she ever wanted. The pictures she had shown Earl were the ones she had been able to hide from Earl's father, who did everything he could to obliterate any memories of her family and her identity.

She had shown him pictures of his great-grandmother, grandparents, aunts, and cousins. Earl had never met any of them. His father had made Rose cut off all connection with her family and moved her far away from them.

He loved one of those pictures in particular. It was of his mother, dressed in a long dress that accentuated her slim waist. Her long black hair piled at the top of her head in an elegant bun. On her neck, she had pearls and she wore long silken gloves. She was smiling and looking radiant, her skin pale and healthy, with not a scar on her.

Now, she was a shell of a human being. He looked at her and could barely see the woman in the picture. It was hard to believe that the woman walking out of the house was the same as the woman in the picture.

His mother suddenly stopped walking and crumpled to the ground. Before long, Earl could hear her deep sobs filling the air. He felt helpless to do anything about it and became agitated. He started to hit his head with his fist.

Thump, thump, thump, thump, thump, thump, thump.
Thump, thump, thump, thump, thump, thump, thump.

Then he began to moan and rock himself, hugging his arms around himself. His mother stopped sobbing immediately after she heard him and shuffled towards the tree she knew he would be hiding in.

"Hey, Earl. Stop it. Look at me, and I am okay." She said, waving her arms up and down, trying to calm him down. He could see her wince whenever she raised her arms although she put on a wide smile on her face. She slowly approached him with arms stretched towards him. She tried to be careful, knowing that Earl was funny about being touched.

She slowly pulled him into her arms and hugged him for all she was worth, even though he remained limp in her arms. They sat that way for what seemed like hours before his mother started to talk about a time before now when things had been better. She had told him all these things before, but Earl sat down on the ground beside her and just listened.

"I know you wonder why I am here and not with my family. I met your father when I turned eighteen. He had come to work on our estate as a gardener. Tall, blue-eyed, and very handsome. I fell head over heels in love with him. Your father was not always like this. We went to church all the time when we first got married." His mother explained, a distant look in her eyes.

"I became pregnant with your sister within three months of meeting your father. My parents were disappointed but were willing to accept him as a son-in-law. We got married right away and had a small cottage on my father's estate, with all that we could ever need for a new couple with nothing. But Tom became antsy and dissatisfied and wanted to leave the estate." Rose continued, looking at her son, her eyes pleading for him to understand.

Earl could not understand. She herself did not understand her own decision.

"We finally moved away from my parent's estate. Tom wasn't always like this. He was loving, attentive and the best person I could ever have had as a husband; although he would get drunk occasionally, he never raised his hands on me. That was before we moved away." Earl sat on his mother's side as she narrated the story.

"Then we moved away, and I gave birth to Ann and the trouble began. And I still stayed because I still loved your father then because he threatened to take my kids away from me. Then finally, I stayed because I have nowhere to go. I have not spoken with my family for years and I don't know if they even remember me. We did not part on good ground." Her voice broke when she said the last part.

She began to sob again, although she tried to stifle her tears to avoid agitating Earl.

"I am sorry, baby. I have not been able to protect you or your sister. Now your sister is gone, and we do not know where she is." She said as the tears flowed freely on her face. Earl looked at her but said nothing. He had a lot of anger at his sister for leaving them.

It was all Earl could do not to burst into tears. He had cried himself to tears the first few days after Ann had left home, but he could see why his older sister had run away.

Ann had run away from home the year before. She had not told anyone and just left, just like that. It had been after one particularly vicious episode of beating for an offense no one could remember. The next morning when Earl woke up, Ann was gone. She had finally had enough. Earl hated his sister for leaving him and their mother behind, even though he did not blame her for running away.

Earl would have run away too, but he could not bear to leave his mother behind with his brute of a father.

And he knew she would not leave the man, no matter how evil he was. When they found out that Ann was missing, his father would not go to the police to report her missing and his mother was too sick and weak to leave the house.

That day, Earl had taken the barn cat they had and climbed his tree, the tears pouring out of his eyes. At first, he had cried out of hurt then a fit of anger so huge and dark rose from deep within him. There was a loud roaring in his ears and his heart pounded very fast. He could barely see for the tears. He jumped down from the tree and hit his head seven times with his closed fist. Seven times on his right temple and seven times on his left. Then he snapped.

For a little while, he was in a daze. When he calmed down, he noticed the blood on his arms and was bleeding. The cat had clawed at him, but it was not without reason. Earl's eyes widened in horror at his own actions. He held the bloody cat with his neck wrung in an awkward direction. He had strangled the poor thing and snapped its neck. He dropped the dead animal and watched its body lay there. Bloody and lifeless.

At first, a great sadness welled up inside of him. He could not believe that he had killed the cat with his bare hands, but then Duke perverted his thoughts. He wanted the guilt of his actions to go away and suddenly, they were gone; instead, he felt fascinated. Earl was impressed that he had managed to kill the cat barehanded. He stared at what used to be a cheerful companion for what seemed like an eternity, then finally, he picked the dead cat up.

Strangely, he had not felt any remorse for his actions. He had not felt disgusted looking at the dead animal in his hands. Rather Earl got a rush from it all. He liked the feeling of the life slowly seeping out of the cat.

Earl did not bury the cat. He hung it on the branch above his favorite spot. People would think that was a sick thing to do, but Earl; was paying homage to the dead animal by displaying it where he did so whoever passed by could see it and admire his work.

"Lovely… truly beautiful", Duke cheered. When he did it again, that was all Duke would say.

A year went by, and Earl grew darker. Now, he had lost count of all the defenseless and small animals he had 'accidentally' killed. Anytime he felt angry or helpless, he would often find one. It was not a difficult task for him, they lived at the edge of town and Earl knew his way around the woods. Sometimes, his mother would find their lifeless bodies around the house and look at him strangely, but she never asked him about them. She wanted to believe that her son was incapable of such… evil.

Then one day, they both sat on the ground, leaning their backs on the large tree as they did. It was nothing special; they were simply enjoying each other's company. Both staring off into the space between the tree and their run-down house.

"Don't worry, and this will all soon end." She whispered as she petted him and for the first time ever, Earl heard something that sounded like hope in his mother's voice.

That simple statement managed to soothe the murderous lust within him.

Hope died. Two months followed and nothing was different. The pain that he had to endure did not end like his mother said it would. If change was coming, then it was not soon enough. Earl began to think he was not the only delusional one in the family. His mother must be suffering from delusions too. Could it be hereditary? They still woke up to beatings and yelling and his sister, Ann was still not back.

At least he still had his sanctuary and there was no shortage of animals to 'help' him with his pain. Duke had taken to calling what Earl did to the animals helping. He also said it was a beautiful thing.

"You know we're doing your family a great favor. Especially your mother." Duke said one day.

"How do you mean?"

"These animals… they're just like your mother. They have to die or else your mother would die. We're saving the innocent." Duke said, which did not make a lot of sense to Earl. Duke had always been a master manipulator, or rather Earl was already too far gone. Easy to push. Duke told him what he wanted to hear, and Earl began to see the logic in his delusions. He thought of how his mother had survived the beatings she got daily and concluded that Duke was right. It was the animals; their sacrifice was necessary for mother's sake. Mother would have died from his father's beatings if he had not been 'helping' her. He thought they were all but of a sacrifice in his mother's place.

Early one morning. His father was already blind drunk and was just fixing to get into another of his moods.

"Rose, where you at?" He bellowed, rising from the chair on unsteady legs. Tom Hughes stood up holding on to the dining table. Earl's mother came into the living room, a kitchen rag in her hands. She tried to stay as far away as possible from Tom knowing how easily he could flare up.

Earl stood at the edge of the room and watched.

"Where is my beer?" Tom hollered. Earl saw his mother flinch.

"Tom, you just drank all of it." She said, cowering at the edge of the room.

"You been stealing off of me, taking out of my drink. You and your no-good crazy son been stealing' from me." Tom said, moving closer to Rose; his fisted hand was already raised. He landed a blow on Rose's head, and she crumpled to the ground. Another one landed on her back before she could say another word.

Suddenly there was a loud sound in the room, and everything went silent. Tom turned towards the back of the room where Earl was standing. The look on his face was of disbelief and anger. His mouth was open as if he was about to go below but no sound came out; instead, he gurgled, and a stream of blood dripped out of his mouth.

Tom took a step towards Earl but crumpled to the ground after just one step. His body convulsed a little before finally becoming still. He was dead but before that, the disbelief had left him sober. For the next five minutes, no one moved a muscle. It was as if time stood still. Then Rose seemed to get herself and suddenly jerked off of the ground and ran towards Earl, taking the shotgun away from him and hugging him tight to her bosom.

"What have you done, Earl?" She asked, her whole body shaking from fright. "You killed your father. Oh, God!"

Earl did not say a word. There was no need for words, and the threat against his mother's life was gone. Slowly, before his eyes, he watched the number seven that had been on his father's forehead for years pulse.

"That is the sign that the evil has been purged. Your mother will be safe now." Duke whispered in his ears. Earl allowed his mother to hug him for a little longer before shrugging her arms away and sitting on the ground, his knees to his chest, slowly rocking himself. No matter how much he tried, he could not stop staring at his father's dead body.

Earl was fascinated by how the eyes were rolled back showing only the whites. He was excited by the puddle of blood and the strong scent of iron mixed with alcohol that permeated the air.

Earl did not understand why his mother was frantic and crying. She sat beside the dead body muttering under her breath.

"What am I going to do?" She asked herself over and over again.

Earl thought his mother must have had one too many blows to the head and must be sick. Why wasn't she happier about this?

"She doesn't understand yet. Many people won't understand us or why we have to do what we will do. You have me... I will understand you. That's more than enough." Duke said. Earl kept looking at the body while Duke explained things to him.

"You know, we have been chosen for great things and I have been sent as your guide. You have done what is needed." Duke had told him. Earl did not find it hard to believe as he knew he was different from the others, and he was special. Earl was sure Duke was right. It felt right. When his father had raised his hand on his mother again, Earl knew he could not take it anymore. He knew that he had to set things right. The pain from the recoil felt worth it.

He quietly ran up the stairs, picked up the gun from under his father's bed, and walked back down the stairs. Duke had held his hand as he aimed and fired. The feeling was much like how he felt when he killed those small animals only amplified by a hundred.

He had felt a rush immediately after he had pulled the trigger. He had felt power course through his veins. For once, he was not the oppressed but the oppressor. Earl had watched a documentary at school when he was in the fifth grade. The teacher had shown them how the gates to a dam were opened. The loud sound the water made caught Earl's attention the most. It sounded like the water was excited to be free finally. That was exactly how he felt, watching his father topple over when he had shot him. These days, he seldom went to school, and no one cared if he did or not.

Suddenly, Rose stood up and began to pace.

One… two… three… four… five… six… seven…

Her steps aligned with his counting. Then she turned around, took another seven steps in the opposite direction, and stopped over the corpse. She continued that way for a while before she stopped moving altogether.

"I have got to call the police! They would know what to do." She said and jumped into action. She went out of the house and headed towards the barn, with an old telephone. A few minutes later, she came back into the house, picked up the gun and wiped it down, leaving only her fingerprints on it.

"It'd be easier to explain that I killed him. Everybody knows how cruel Tom was." Her voice cracked when she said his name. He was a monster, but like a faithful wife, she loved him still. Tom was a man once. Once. She went about the room making everything look like she was the one who did it. Earl did not move from where he had been sitting and was still staring at the corpse.

Rose seemed to realize how that would look to the police and went to him and led him out of the house. Earl went willingly enough but kept staring back at the corpse, and she led him to his favorite tree.

"Don't leave this place until I come for you. You hear me, Earl. Everything will be just fine." She said to him and walked back to the house. Earl saw her stand in front of the house, hugging the gun to her chest.

A few minutes later, Earl heard sirens and the police came. It was a while before his mother came for him as she said, and she went with a policeman who held her by the arm.

"Come here, Earl. We will follow this nice policeman, and he will take you to a safe place." She said in that singsong voice she used when she wanted to coerce him to do something he did not want to.

"You are coming too, right mama?" He asked. His mother only nodded and said nothing else.

Earl walked towards them and followed the man. Earl and his mother were placed in an ambulance.

Soon enough, the paramedics carried the dead body out of the house and into another ambulance. Earl watched them place the stretcher in the ambulance through the open door of the ambulance he and his mother were in.

"I wonder if he is heavy," Earl whispered to Duke, who was beside him, careful not to talk too loudly to avoid strange looks from other people. That was the last time Earl ever saw his father.

Rose was given a full examination at the hospital and her wounds were bandaged. A policeman was around her all the time and Earl wondered why. Earl remained in the hospital room with her keeping his mother in sight at all times. She was his only family and he had to protect her.

"May I speak with him alone? Please?" Rose said to the policeman when the nurse had finished cleaning her wounds up. The man looked at her and then Earl before nodding and walking out of the room, gently shutting the door behind him.

"Come here, Earl." His mother's small, raspy voice said. Something was very wrong. He knew it but was not sure what. He thought he had taken care of the situation; his mother was no longer in danger, and she looked like things were even worse.

He walked closer to the bed and stood a foot away. She held her left hand out towards him and gestured for him to come closer. The other was cuffed to the hospital bed.

"I know you were trying to protect me. Now, I can do what a mother's supposed to. I'm sorry I failed to protect you and your sister from your father. I'm sorry." She said, her voice choking up with tears. Earl was confused.

"No momma. It's not your fault. Father had an evil heart, and you were just helpless to do anything about it." He said to her, but she was not listening.

"Oh, baby. I wish you would talk to me. I see you talk but you never speak to me. I wonder who you talk to." She said, still hugging him close to her chest.

"I am talking. It's not you, and I was meant to protect you." He said again, making his voice even louder but she still looked confused and sad.

"She cannot hear you, Earl," Duke said.

"Why can't she hear me?" He turned and asked Duke who just shrugged his shoulders.

Earl's mother burst into deep sobs, seeing him talk to nobody and hating herself for allowing him to go through all he did at the hands of his father all those years. She believed his mind had become messed up because of that.

A knock sounded at the door.

"Everything alright in there?" The policeman asked from outside.

"Yes, sir. Everything is fine." His mother answered.

She then turned to him and looked at him, an urgent look in her eyes.

"Now listen to me, Earl. Momma's going away for a little while. You can never tell anyone what really happened this morning, and no one would understand you. You are momma's big helper. Be a good boy for momma, would you?" She said, holding his head between her frail hands.

Earl did not know what to do but nodded his head.

"I will be back to get you." She said finally. Earl wondered where she might be going. They needed to stick together.

"Your mother is leaving you too. She hates you just like your father did and she thinks you're a burden. After everything we'd done for her." Duke's voice whispered into his ears. Earl scowled with so much hate.

"That's not true. We are going to be together forever, and she is not going anywhere." Earl said to Duke. He heard his mother's sobs increase and he turned toward her.

"Who are you talking to, baby? Talk to me. I will be back for you, I promise." She said, responding to the question in his eyes.

He wanted to talk but then he paled. Fear gripped his heart like no other. It was like a cold wind had blown over him, one cold enough to freeze hell and slowly, the number seven materialized on her forehead. Earl drew back from her. The number faded in and out as tears rose in his eyes. 'No…No…No…' he refused to accept it.

"Mama, where are you going?" He asked in a small voice, hoping that Duke was lying. His mother could not speak; just shut her eyes, allowing the welled-up tears to roll down her cheeks.

The pain in his chest was so excruciating, and it felt like someone had taken a vice to his ribs and was squeezing him. His head began to pound and his heart raced. Earl could hear his mother's voice calling out for him somewhere in the distance.

"Earl, baby. Calm down. I will come to see you as soon as I get out." She was saying but the roar in his ears grew even louder.

"She is leaving. Just like your sister left you." Duke whispered in Earl's ears. He began to shake his head. Unknown to him, he was banging his head against the wall.

Thump, thump, thump, thump, thump, thump, thump.
Thump, thump, thump, thump, thump, thump, thump.

"Somebody, help me! Help my baby!" Rose screamed, watching in horror as her son bang his head on the wall. She tried to jump out of the hospital bed but did not get far as her hand had been cuffed to the bed. The door burst open, and the policeman walked in just as he slumped to the floor unconscious catching him before he could hit his head on the floor.

"What happened to him, ma'am?" He asked, wincing at the gash on the boy's head.

"He became upset and started to bang his head against the wall. He has been like this since he was three." Rose explained just as the doctor walked into the room.

"Have you had him checked and tested for any mental disorders?" The elderly doctor asked her.

"No, sir." Rose said while shaking her head. The doctor continued to examine him before a stretcher was brought in and Earl was wheeled out.

"Where are y'all taking him to?" Rose asked frantically.

"We are taking him to get examined and cleaned up. The wound is quite serious, and you say he was banging his head against the wall? We need to be sure there is no permanent or serious damage." The doctor explained, which seemed to calm Rose down.

EARL WOKE UP SLOWLY, CONFUSED. IT WAS STILL LIGHT outside, and he was not sure where he was or what had happened. He tried to look around, but his head felt heavy. There was another bed in the room occupied by another boy who looked younger than Earl. His mother stood over his bed, fluffing the pillows.

"Do you need anything, baby?" Earl could hear the woman ask the boy, who shook his head quietly. Earl envied him, and he wished his mother was there with him too.

"Momma…" he called but his voice only came out in a whisper. Suddenly, Duke was there.

"She's gone and you know it. She's gone forever." He said to Earl, a sad smile on his face. Earl closed his eyes and opened them again. Duke was still there but nothing had changed. Earl stared up at a white ceiling with harsh white lights. His head hurt and his mouth was dry.

A nurse walked into the room.

"Ahh, you are awake." She said, her voice loud and cheerful. She smiled at the other woman and boy before facing him fully. The nurse was beautiful and had blonde hair and lips which were painted a deep red. It looked like blood was dripping off of her lips. Earl blinked and took his eyes away from her lips.

"Where's my momma?" He asked the nurse.

"Oh, honey. Your momma's been taken away." She said, a look of pity coming over her beautiful face.

"But don't worry. Someone is coming to take good care of you and place you in a good place. And I will do my best to see that your head is better. And I am sure your momma's going to be back very soon." She quickly said, when she noticed that he had begun to breathe quickly and become restless again.

"She's lyin.' Your momma's gone and you will never see her again in your life. She wasn't grateful for what we did and wants nothing to do with you. You saw the mark on her, didn't you?" Duke asked him.

"That's not true. She's telling the truth! You are a liar, Duke!" Earl shouted back at Duke. A strange look came over the woman's face, but she quickly hid it when she saw him looking at her. Her smile grew wider than ever. Unnervingly so.

The woman at the other side of the room also turned to look at him. Her face had gone pale, and she looked from him to the nurse and then around the room as if to see if there was another person with them. Then she turned and faced her son, her back towards him.

"See, everyone thinks you're crazy, just like your father did. Maybe you are," Duke said and cackled with laughter. Earl shook his head, counting to seven in his head and slowly tapping his leg and exhaling as he counted.

One…Two…Three…

Earl began to count under his breath.

"Oh. Do you want to ignore me and make yourself believe I don't exist? You know it never works. I'll always be here; I'll always be back. You need me." Duke said, a taunting tone in his voice.

Four… Five… Six… Seven…

By the time he finished counting, Duke was no longer in the room, only the beautiful nurse with the bright smile was there.

An elderly man stuck his head into the room and gestured for the nurse to come. She smiled at Earl and went towards the man. They stepped out but did not close the door all the way so Earl could hear what they were saying.

"The police have notified the Child Protective Services and they will send a social worker very soon. The mother has been taken to jail." The man said while the woman nodded.

Jail? Was his mother in jail? Earl thought, tears springing up in his eyes.

"Doctor, I noticed earlier that he was talking to someone but there was no one in the room." The woman said. The man she called doctor nodded and they both looked into the room. Earl had his eyes closed so they must have assumed that he had fallen back asleep.

"Yes, his mother did say he used to talk to imaginary people and do things in bizarre ways. I have my suspicions but since they never got a diagnosis, it would be best if we got the professionals to check him. We can transfer him to the department of Psychiatry before the social worker gets here." The man said while the woman nodded.

Mental health? Did they think he was crazy too? Earl thought. He heard the door open, and the nurse walked back into the room. Immediately she came in, his roommate's mother quickly went out, glancing briefly at him. She quickly averted her eyes when she saw him looking at her.

"Doctor…!" She called after the elderly man who had spoken with the nurse. The man turned and looked at her, a smile on his face.

"Hello, Mrs. Dale. I believe your son is responding to treatment." Earl heard the doctor ask her. She nodded but then started to talk in a low tone, gesturing towards him all the while. Earl knew she was talking about him and not good things from the look on her face.

"Don't worry, Earl. You will feel better very soon." The nurse said to him, still smiling. He turned away from her towards the wall and refused to talk.

The nurse left a little while later and Earl sat up slowly and got a good look at the room. The walls were painted cheerful yellow, which was ironic because he felt anything but cheerful, and he hated this room.

The other occupant of the room looked at him and smiled but Earl did not smile back. His mother had still not returned.

"Hi." The boy said in a small voice.

"Hello," Earl replied just before the boy's mother walked in. Earl immediately turned away from the boy, who was not-so-quietly reprimanding her son for talking to him.

CHAPTER

SIX

E arl woke up early the next morning and sat up in the bed. The boy who had been in the room with him was no longer in the room. Sometime in the night, they must have moved him out. His mother must have gotten what she wanted. Earl shrugged his shoulders like he did not care. The nurse from yesterday came in, checked his charts, and took his temperature. Two people went into the room after he had been given breakfast. One of them was the doctor from the day before. Earl was sitting up when they walked into the room.

"Hello, Earl. My name is Dr. Elvin. How do you feel?" The man from earlier asked, his voice cheerful.

"Fine, thank you," Earl said politely.

"Good. This is Dr. Mia Thompson. She will examine you further to make sure you are better." The doctor said, gesturing to the other woman with him.

"You think I am crazy, right?" Earl asked quietly, a nonchalant look on his face. Dr. Elvin could see that it was only a front as his body was tense and knew that whatever answer they gave would mean a lot to him.

"Oh no. We do not think you are crazy, and I will not insult you by playing semantics with you. I can see that you are a bright young man." The woman said to him. Earl nodded and sat up even straighter. He liked that she was not talking down at him. He was not a child and knew more than they thought he did.

"We have made some observations in addition to what your mother has told us. There are some things we need to be sure about which may have been caused by the way you grew up. My team and I would like to help you in any way we can." She explained to him. Earl liked the sound of that but tried not to get too excited. Things could still go wrong very wrong, and he could not trust anyone.

"Whatever." He said and shrugged, trying to look like he did not care. The doctors looked at each other and tried to engage Earl in further conversation.

Before the day ran out, Earl had to undergo many tests and answer many questions. Dr. Thompson explained all the tests and questionnaires to him as they were being administered; even though he did not understand most of what she said to him, Earl pretended he understood. He liked being talked to like an adult, not a child.

A woman who the nurse said was the social worker from the Child Protective Services came later that day. She was a middle-aged woman with tired-looking eyes. She introduced herself as Miss Horowitz. He found her name strange and tried hard not to laugh. She was kind and soft spoken. She told him about his mother, but Earl pretended he did not care. His mother had left him, and it did not matter to him that she had no choice and had to be put in jail. All he knew was that she had left him. Alone.

"So, we would be moving you to home until your mother comes to get you. A lovely couple would take good care of you. You would have young people your age to be with and go to school with." Miss Horowitz informed him. Earl did not know how to feel about that. Duke was the only other person outside of his family that Earl knew and had been his only friend. Earl was not sure what having other people his age would be like.

Almost everyone he had known his age had been cruel to him, and he was sure this was going to be the case anywhere he was taken. He had learned that one can be lonely even in a room full of people, especially when they were considered different.

"Can't I just stay with my momma? I promise I will be a good boy." Earl said to Miss Horowitz. The woman smiled at him compassionately.

"No, Earl. You cannot stay with your momma, and she is going to come for you as soon as she can. Young men cannot be where she is." She told him, and Earl did not understand that and felt lonely.

He had not heard Duke since the day before. Earl liked that his head was quiet, but he still missed Duke. Sometimes he did that. Just up and disappeared. He would do that anytime Earl disagreed with him about something. Duke must still be angry that Earl had called him a liar. One thing Earl was sure of was that Duke would surely come around. Sooner or later.

The social worker left after informing him that she would be back for him the next day and that he should get ready. Earl could not sleep for the fear and trepidation he felt even though he tried not to show it. He had an inkling of what to expect, which was the scariest part.

When it was morning, the nurse came in and checked his head then gave him some food.

"I see you are going home today." The nurse said, smiling at Earl brightly. He nodded his head but remained silent.

"You do not look excited. Well, I believe you will enjoy yourself if you just allow yourself. Now, don't go around getting upset and banging your head on walls any longer. I want you to be healthy. You hear me?" She said to him, looking directly into his face. Earl's ears grew hot then he averted his eyes and nodded.

"That's a good boy." The nurse said and left the room. Miss. Horowitz walked in just then, holding a thin file in her hands.

"Good morning, Earl. I hope you had a wonderful night?" She said cheerily. A bit too cheerily for his liking.

She looked less tired today than she did yesterday. Earl nodded but did not say anything.

"Well, I am going to take you to the family who is going to take care of you for the mean time. I believe you are ready to go. We need to leave immediately." She explained while helping Earl get off the bed. Earl picked up a garbage disposal bag that contained his few belongings which consisted of two shirts, a pair of trousers and an old pair of shoes. His mother had packed them before they had left home two days ago with the police.

Miss. Horowitz allowed him to walk ahead of her as they stepped out of the room. They passed by the nurses' station where the nurse who had attended to him was sitting writing in a file.

She raised her head and smiled when she saw him.

"Aww baby, you are leaving'? Bye, Earl." She said, making him blush again. He shyly waved his hand at her and quickly walked out with the social worker. They got into a beat-up blue Volkswagen that seemed to have seen better days on the outside.

The inside was even worse than the outside. The whole car looked as if it was one mile away from falling apart. The seats were threadbare, and Miss. Horowitz had so many files and papers stacked in her car.

"Sorry for the mess." She said, trying to free up the passenger seat for him. Earl sat in the seat when a small, cleared space appeared and held his belongings in his lap. Miss Horowitz started the old engine and asked him to put on his seatbelt, and he did and they began the drive.

Earl slept off while she drove and only woke up when the car stopped moving. He opened his eyes when Miss and Horowitz stopped the car engine, and she had stopped the car at the side of the road.

"You are awake. We are almost at Milk Ranch, Naperville where the Johnsons live. You can stretch your legs if you want." She informed him, picking up a file from the back of the car. She stretched her legs before getting back into the driver's seat. He decided not to stretch his legs and remained in the car.

Earl had never been out of Crest Hill in his life and did not know anything about Naperville.

"I will give you a background on them, so you know what you are going to meet there." She said, starting the engine and pulling into the road again.

Earl nodded, trying to clear his eyes' last cobwebs of sleep. The medicine Dr. Thompson had begun to give him made him groggy all the time. She had told him after the series of tests that he had something called atypical autism presenting with psychosis. She explained it to him, but Earl did not understand what she was saying.

"…Johnson is a full-time farmer, and his wife is a stay-at-home mom. There are four other kids your age on their farm. So, you would not lack any company. Besides, since you grew up on a farm, it would not be entirely strange for you." Miss Horowitz said, looking up at him with a smile. Earl did not smile back. Instead, he turned his head away from her and began to rock himself back and forth.

He had not been excited about meeting new people but to hear that he was going to a farm to meet complete strangers and even live with them made it worse. What if they were all like his father had been?

"Umm…Earl? Everything will be alright. No need to get agitated." Miss. Horowitz told him, careful not to touch him. She continued the drive and they were at the Johnson farm in less than thirty minutes.

"We are here." She said and opened her door. Earl remained in the car, staring up at the old farmhouse. It was no different from his father's house except that it was in better shape and looked like it was cleaner. It was also very big, way bigger than where he had grown up.

Earl could see the barn just behind the house to the right and a grove of trees on the left-hand side. At the other side of the barn was what looked like a paddock with a few horses running around.

Two adults and four young people, two girls and two boys, stood on the porch, all dressed in coveralls. They all had broad smiles on their faces too. The man, very tall with a wide shoulder, walked down the porch steps and approached Miss. Horowitz shook her hand vigorously.

"Mr. Johnson! Thank you for having us." Miss. Horowitz said.

"The pleasure is all ours, ma'am. Nice to be able to be of help." He said in a soft, high-pitched voice that surprised Earl. He had never heard a man have such a small voice before. His father's voice had been loud and booming, filling their small house whenever he spoke, especially when he had been drinking.

The woman, squat and fat but with a pleasant looking face, joined her husband and Miss Horowitz and they began to speak with each other, glancing at him in the car occasionally.

Earl began to rock himself in the small space, beginning to feel anxious about being left in the care of these people. What if the man turned out to be just like his father?

A sound that seemed to be coming from afar started to grow louder and louder until he had to place his hands on his ears to block the sound.

"One… Two… Three… Four… Five… Six… Seven…" He counted under his breath while tapping his thigh. Gradually, the sound died down and he could hear himself breathe again. The car door suddenly jerked open, and the buxom woman was at his side smiling at him.

"Come on out, dear." She said, opening the door wider for Earl to come out. He refused to budge, and the woman looked up at Miss Horowitz with a confused gaze. The social worker came to the car and spoke gently to him.

"Hey, Earl. This is Mrs. Johnson and her husband. They own and run the Milk Ranch and they will be taking care of you from now on. I will be checking up on you occasionally too." She said, crouching beside the door. Earl did not look at any of their faces as he stepped out of the car, still holding his plastic bag tightly in his hands.

Mrs. Johnson gestured for him to follow her and walked in front of him, her husband and the social worker coming behind them. Earl took slow, deliberate steps towards the large porch where the four children were still standing. The oldest looked like he would not be much more than sixteen years old, and the youngest girl looked ten.

He sized each of them up, trying to see if he had any advantage over any of them. He would need to know how to protect himself if they tried something funny. His experience with people taught him that kids could be just as cruel as drunk adult.

Mrs. Johnson gestured to the four children, still smiling broadly at Earl.

"These are Henry, Neil, Sarah and Molly." Pointing to each one as she called their names. Earl did not look directly at them but set his gaze directly above their heads.

"Henry is seventeen and the oldest boy, followed by Sarah. She is sixteen while Neil is fourteen. Molly is our baby, and she is ten." Mrs. Johnson said.

Henry had blond hair and blue eyes. Sarah was a plain-looking girl with mousy brown hair and a shy look about her. Neil's black hair was curly and looked like a bird's nest. He had freckles scattered across his face. He wore thick, wire-rimmed glasses and looked like he would not be able to see a thing without them.

On the other hand, Molly was the friendliest-looking kid among them. Her smile looked like it was coming from deep within her heart. She was pretty with long eyelashes and blonde hair.

They all said, "Nice to meet you." But Earl did not respond, and he did not trust them one bit.

"Come on in. I am going to show you to your room." Mr. Johnson said in his thin voice, leading the way into the house. Earl walked behind the man. It took a little while for his eyes to become accustomed to the inside, and it was a bit dark.

The living room was large and was decorated in a way strange to Earl but comfortable. Somehow, he knew that this was how a home was meant to be.

You cannot let yourself be comfortable here. Finally, Duke said something.

They went up the stairs where there were four rooms. They paused at the first room just opposite the stairs.

"This is the room Sarah and Molly share. You and the boys will share the next room." Mr. Johnson said, leading him to the said room. It had two bunk beds, one already occupied by the other two boys. He could tell by the fact that the beds were made.

The room had its own bathroom, something Earl had never seen yet, and he was used to using the outhouse on his father's farm.

"You can choose either to stay on the top bunk or the bottom. Feel free here." Mrs. Johnson said, bringing sheets and blankets along with her, and she handed them over to him and gently pushed him into the room.

"You set yourself up and come downstairs when you are done for lunch." She said as they all turned, leaving him in the room alone. He could hear their voices but did not hear everything they were saying, and he imagined they were talking about him.

He caught snippets of their conversation.

"…he has to be on medication…mental instability… nightmares" were among what he heard.

Earl suddenly grew angry, hating being here and not wanting this to be home. He wanted his momma. He sat on the bed without laying the sheets and looked up. He could see the ceiling through the slats of the upper bunk. It was painted a pale blue, and someone had drawn clouds on the ceiling.

He hissed and turned on his side, facing the wall. He began to cry and did not know when he fell asleep. He forgot his pain for a short while, but the anger remained.

All he knew was the anger.

THE NEXT MORNING, MRS. JOHNSON WOKE HIM UP FOR breakfast. She had put extra effort into his. "Hey, Earl. Time for breakfast then homeschool." Mrs. Johnson called him with a smile. He looked around the room and the other boys were no longer in the room.

"I am not hungry and do not want to be homeschooled." He retorted, turning his back on her. He wanted to be stubborn, and after he was sure she was only pretending to be nice.

"Well, that is too bad, but you will have breakfast and come to the study for homeschool, or I will camp out here and not let you be." She told him. He caught a hint of mirth in her voice and wondered what she found funny. He was not going to budge, he decided. They could beat him up and even starve him, but he would live on his own terms on this ranch, and they could not make him do anything.

The woman left the room and quietly closed her door a few minutes later. He was ready for anything.

A moment later, Mr. Johnson entered the room. His tall frame filling the room. Earl refused to turn away from the wall, sure he was in for a beating but when the man did not speak or move after a few minutes, he moved his head slightly so he could see him.

Mr. Johnson was holding a tray in his hands and was looking down at him.

"I said I did not want to eat anything!" Earl shouted angrily. Just then, his stomach decided to growl. Mr. Johnson looked at Earl's stomach and chuckled.

"I reckon your stomach feels otherwise." He said, moving away from the door and into the room. He drew one of the chairs away from the study table closer to Earl and settled the tray on it. Earl looked at the tray and his mouth watered.

The plate was heaped with a large helping of pancakes covered with more syrup than Earl had seen in his life. A glass of orange juice sat beside the plate. He looked at it hungrily then looked up at Mr. Johnson. Seeing the mirth in his face, Earl turned towards the wall, trying to ignore him.

His stomach growled again.

"Well, when you get around to feeding the demon in your belly, you can bring the tray and the plates down to the kitchen." Mr. Johnson said and quietly walked out of the room.

Earl waited for a few minutes before sitting up.

There was no need to starve. If he had to stay here, he could eat their food, and it does not change anything.

He finished all the food within minutes and contemplated whether to take the plate down as instructed or not.

He had better take the plates down, and he would not want them not to feed him again. When he got downstairs with the tray, he stood at the foot of the stairs, unsure where to go. He did not know where the kitchen was.

Mrs. Johnson came out just then. She smiled when she noticed him.

"Well, look who it is." She said and took the tray from him. "Did you enjoy breakfast?" She asked him. Earl nodded.

"Good. Come with me." She said and Earl followed her into the kitchen. It was large like almost every room in the house. She placed the tray in the sink and took some cans from the cupboard.

"You have to take your medications now." She said, shaking a few of the pills into her hands and handing them to him. He reluctantly swallowed them, which satisfied her as she smiled at him.

Neil came into the kitchen just then.

"We are ready ma'am." He said to Mrs. Johnson.

"Alright. Show Earl to the study, will you?" She instructed Neil, who gestured for Earl to follow him, pushing his glasses up the bridge of his nose. Earl followed him to the study, where the others were already seated waiting for lessons to start.

Neil pointed him to a seat at the end of the room, closest to Molly, and Earl sat in it looking straight ahead.

"Hi, Earl." Molly said in a small voice. He ignored her and continued to look straight ahead.

Mr. Johnson came into the room and lessons continued. Earl did not have trouble catching up. He had always been a quick learner and since he actually liked reading, he enjoyed lessons.

After lessons, Mr. Johnson assigned everyone tasks. Earl's tasks were to work with Henry to take care of the horses and their stalls.

He followed Henry to the paddock where the horses were being kept. The pleasant expression on Henry's face became sour immediately they were out of Mr. Johnson's sight, and Henry did not say anything to Earl until they got to the paddock.

He pointed at the shovel asking Earl to pick it up, then pointed him to a stall.

"Clean it up!" He said and promptly sat down. Earl picked up the shovel and walked to the stall Henry had pointed at. He quietly started cleaning the stall and finished within minutes. He surveyed his work and was pleased with what he had done. He looked satisfied with himself. He came out of the stall.

"I am done." He said to Henry who had been dozing.

"No, you are not," Henry said, pointing at the other stalls, seven in total. "You have to do all."

"What will you be doing?" Earl asked.

"How is that your business? Who do you think you are asking me questions, you crazy piece of shit?" Henry said, standing up and shoving Earl in the chest. Earl lost his balance and fell on his backside. Henry was much bigger than Earl and easily overpowered him

"If you ever take that attitude with me again, I am going to beat the living shit out of you." He said, bringing his face close to Earl's face.

"And you try telling anybody. No one is going to believe you." Henry said with a smirk. "Now get off your ass and do as you have been told. I am not going to repeat myself."

Earl quietly got up and mucked the remaining seven stalls. He had almost finished cleaning the last stall when Mr. Johnson came into the paddock, and Henry quickly shoved him out and continued to clean it as if he had been doing that all the while.

"Good job, boys!" The man said.

"Thank you, sir!" Henry replied, looking at Earl as if daring him to say anything. Earl kept his mouth shut, knowing that this was just the beginning of a long and painful life. Nothing new there.

Life at the Milk Ranch quickly took on a routine, and one Earl gradually got used to. He liked it. The only thing making it sour was the way Henry treated him and the other kids when the Johnsons were not watching. Earl did his best not to react, but the anger was there, growing into a solid mass in his chest.

Mrs. Johnson was big on the Bible and liked to teach them stories from the Bible, making them say prayers and such.

"You know kids, and there are seven deadly sins. Pride is the gravest of them all. The Lord says he opposes the proud. Who can stand being opposed by God, a consuming fire? Anyone who does go to hell, no negotiation. The only redemption they have is death." She taught them, her eyes filled with such fierceness; Earl was afraid she could cause the bible she was holding to burst into flames.

"There is the deadly sin of envy. I will not hesitate to take a switch to any of you, who is prone to envy, and I do not encourage it." She continued. Neil turned and looked at Harry, accusation in his eyes. Earl totally agreed with him.

Mrs. Johnson went on to list the remaining deadly sins, telling them why they should avoid them. They heard about the perils of being proud, envious, wrathful, gluttonous, greedy, lustful, or slothful. Each child was given just enough food to avoid gluttony, and food privileges were taken away from anyone who seemed unsatisfied.

One day, Mrs. Johnson caught Henry with a magazine with nude women on it. That day, he slept in the barn. Earl was happy at the justice of it.

Mr. Johnson was a quiet man. His wife ran the home more than he did and Earl got a sense that he preferred it that way.

Every day for the next three years, Earl learned about the reality of hellfire and condemnation for wrongdoing. He did not mind at all. Mrs. Johnson only spoke the truth, and justice had to be served.

The seven deadly sins and their consequences struck a chord in Earl's young heart.

Earl lived on the Milk Ranch for a whole year doing Henry's chores and enduring insults from him. He did everything he was asked to do without complaining. Earl became fairly comfortable with Mr. Johnson and his wife and even became friends with Sarah, Neil, and Molly.

On the other hand, Henry remained a thorn in his flesh, and it was all Earl could do not to explode. The other kids were also afraid of him, but no one said anything to the Johnsons.

Earl hated his medications but kept taking them. They always left him feeling murky and sometimes disoriented. So, some days when Mrs. Johnson was not watching, he would throw the drugs away. On those days, he would feel much sharper and be more energetic.

He was sure the Johnsons noticed the changes in his mood, but they did not say anything about it. Mrs. Johnson just chalked it up to him becoming more comfortable with staying with them.

Those were also the days when Earl could hear Duke's voice.

"I hate Henry," Duke said on one of such days after Earl and Neil had just finished their chores. They had also done Henry's chores while he sat around doing nothing but calling them names. The anger rose up in Earl's chest and he heard a loud roaring sound in his ears.

"I will soon turn eighteen. Then I can leave here, and I can leave you two dorks and go on with my life." He spoke. Then he would brag about how many things he was going to do once he was free.

Earl wondered how he got away with being a jerk. He was always the good kid when the Johnsons were around. Mrs. Johnson even used him as a behavioral model for them.

If only she knew.

"Hey, Earl. Come here!" Henry called for him one day while they were doing chores in the barn. As usual, Henry had handed his chores to the two younger boys and was sitting around doing nothing. Earl approached him warily. The way you would approach a wild cat, careful to avoid being scratched and bitten.

"Go and bring me some water. I am thirsty." He spoke.

"But I'm busy." Earl retorted. Doing your chores, he thought but did not say out loud. Immediately as he said that, Henry stood up from where he had been sitting and grabbed Earl by the collar, holding him tightly around the neck, enough to cut his air supply.

Earl struggled, gasping for air, and was becoming lightheaded.

"What have I said about talking back at me?" Henry asked, still holding Earl around the neck.

Duke had enough, and he was not going to take it any longer.

"AARRRGGGGHHH..." An unearthly sound came out of Earl's mouth as he struggled for breath. Earl did not know when he lifted his hands or how he had managed to get a firm grip around Henry's neck. For a moment, he was not himself. The rage in Henry's eyes was short-lived. Slowly, Henry's grip around Earl's collar loosened, causing him to release Earl. With new breath in his lungs, Earl was glad he was free, but he was not satisfied. He shoved his weight forward and in a blink, Henry was pinned to the stall wall gasping for breath and crying as he was being strangled. Henry's eyes turned red and began to bulge out of their sockets, almost like they would pop out. His breathing came in gasps. He was struggling to get Earl's hands away from around his neck but was unable. Henry was losing consciousness.

Neil, who was also in the barn, froze, unable to believe what he was seeing.

"DON'T YOU EVER LAY HANDS ON US AGAIN." Earl whispered in a raspy and menacing voice. Henry's face had begun to turn blue with tears and dread in his red eyes as he struggled for breath and flailed his arms weakly.

"Stop it! You're hurting him!" Neil shouted, pushing his glasses up the bridge of his nose and running towards Earl to pull his hands away from Henry, and his tiny hands could not manage it. Instead, Earl laughed very uncharacteristically, and he was enjoying himself.

"Earl, please stop," Neil begged.

"That will put the fear of God in you, spineless bully."

'Sorry...' Henry croaked as his eyes rolled back and Earl seemed to regain his senses at that point. He gasped loudly as he quickly released Henry and stepped away from him in shock. Henry fell limply to the ground but regained himself in a couple of seconds then curled up in a ball scrambling away from Earl. Earl looked down at his hands as if seeing them for the first time and turned his gaze to Henry in disbelief.

Henry could not look up at him. He remained as far away as possible from Earl.

"I'm sorry, Henry. I didn't mean to get angry." Earl said, walking closer to Henry. Henry shrunk back, becoming even smaller. Neil threw himself between to help Henry.

"Don't come near me!" He screamed, stopping Earl in his tracks.

Neil could not speak and though he rushed to Henry, he could not help but see Earl in a different light. In Neil's eyes, there was a newfound respect for Earl but there was also fear.

"Fear me. A healthy dose of fear is all you deserve," Duke gloated.

Within two weeks, Henry was off the farm. Luckily, the bruises on his neck went unnoticed but that was not the case. The Johnsons had noticed a change in his behavior and had called his caseworker. He was no longer his cheerful self and was always subdued. Henry would not eat but instead cowered in a corner. He was suddenly becoming unhealthy, and the Johnsons did not know how to help him. It was very unusual. But Henry refused to talk about it.

It troubled them dearly, but the cause of Henry's abnormality was no mystery to the other kids. The other kids knew the truth behind it, but no one said a thing. For once, they did not have Henry breathing threats and insults down their necks. And as selfish as that was, they were satisfied with how things turned out.

After Henry left the ranch, the Johnsons had not taken any more foster kids. The CPC thought it suspicious that the boy's personality would change drastically in such a short time but since he would not say anything to warrant it, an investigation into the Johnsons and the remaining kids turned up nothing against them. The Johnsons were good people and there was no proof of abuse, so they left the four kids in their care.

Mr. Johnson had hired an additional hand to help around the ranch since his wife was not feeling too well and the kids could only do so much. Kevin Boyd, the new help was a dark, handsome, fun-loving, and quiet guy. He was 19 years old but looked much older cause of the beard he was so proud of and loved to play games with them. Other than that, when he played with them, he went about his business without interfering with anyone else. He was a diligent worker, and Earl respected that about him before Sarah turned eighteen. As always, you left Johnson's home at eighteen because then you would be considered a full-fledged adult. Sarah did not want to leave, rather she wanted to stay and help at the house with all the other kids and the Johnsons did not mind the idea, in fact, they were willing to pay her as well if she did.

Earl had grown close to the other kids since Henry left. They were kind to him, and they had become as close as siblings could get. It did not matter that there was no blood between them. Those had been the best years of his life. He was happy taking his medication and doing as Mr. and Mrs. Johnson said. There was no Duke in his paradise. His social worker would go months without having to visit him. There was no need for visits, and he was doing well enough with no complaints about his once destructive behavior.

Just before Sarah turned eighteen, Earl noticed she had become close with this newly hired help. Too close in fact. He was not worried at first but honestly a bit jealous, so he tried to keep them apart as subtly as he could manage. He was fond of the help but could not shake unease about the man. The thought of them together kept stirring up thoughts of his mother, about her ordeal with Tom Hughes, his father. As she said, Tom was a good man once; Earl had no intention of learning how good Kevin was.

Their innocent chatting turned into flirting and had been going on for a while before Earl had to talk to Sarah. Rather than listening to him, she got pissed and told him off. Earl was hurt but he could not blame her; instead, it was his fault for not approaching the matter delicately. So, he devised a new approach that did not directly involve her. Earl kept a close eye on Kevin. He wanted to know just the kind of guy he was off grounds and even resorted to following him into town when he had the chance. He did not learn much though, not that he had hoped to find anything incriminating in the first place. He was just being careful and now he knew where Kevin lived. From his little trips after Kevin, he began to learn his way around town; it made it easier to tail him unnoticed. They seldom had a need to be in the main town except to go to church on Sundays with the

Johnsons. They provided all that they needed. Now Earl wondered if he was pushing his luck. He concluded he was overacting and decided to leave it be.

One day, Earl was feeling adventurous and ran into the barn. He, Sarah, and Kevin were meant to run a few errands but since he had not seen them, he decided he would play hooky. He regretted it. It was a flux but actually, he caught Sarah and Kevin having sex there. Earl was startled but so were they. He intended to run off, but Sarah begged him to hear them out first. They begged him not to tell the Johnsons about them. Sarah and Kevin were in love with each other.

"Kevin loves me and I love him too. Please don't tell them. They would not understand and would try to separate us." Sarah pleaded with him.

"Believe us… I'd do anything for your sister." Kevin added. Earl was reluctant; he felt they were more afraid of punishment than being separated. He would have reported them but in the end, he did not see a point in being a snitch. Earl wanted to believe that they were truly in love with each other. He agreed to keep their secret and the two could rest easy. From that day, Earl became overly conscious of his surroundings. He did not hate Kevin but always kept a keen eye on him. He might have just been paranoid but a part of him felt moved to watch Kevin.

A few weeks later, Sarah discovered she was pregnant. She did not hesitate immediately to tell Kevin soon as she was certain. She was scared out of her mind but also very happy. She had always dreamt of being a mother. She believed that since they loved each other, she and Kevin could get married and have their baby. Then live happily ever after.

Sarah was naive. They were far too young; Kevin did not take the news likely. "What are you saying?" He snapped bewilderedly, "Do you have any idea what you've done? I'm not going to marry you- it's your fault for being dumb and getting knocked up."

Earl watched. He heard the whole thing and saw Sarah's mouth drop open in disbelief. Her face contorted in surprised anger. "What're you saying, Kevin? You said you loved me. Why are you being so cruel? Isn't this what we wanted?"

Sarah was hurt but still wanted to believe in Kevin.

Neither of them knew Earl was listening in. It was almost fated that it was in the barn he had discovered them that their little dialogue was held, and this time Earl was not going to let himself be discovered. He had not intended to eavesdrop on them; rather he was there long before they arrived. He hid when he saw them come in and so he continued hiding, listening to their argument. He stepped out of the shadows when he felt the argument was becoming violent and just in time to see, Kevin had raised his hand to Sarah.

Earl was disappointed in them both but in Kevin even more. Kevin turned on his heel and left Sarah sobbing; he did not want to cause a scene. Earl gritted his teeth angry at what he had just stopped from happening. His mother came to mind again.

He had not gone to visit her at the prison since he had been put with the Johnsons, and though he would not admit it, Earl was still of the mind that his mother had abandoned him. He sat beside Sarah on the ground until she calmed down.

"What am I going to do?" She asked him, and Earl did not have any answers so all he did was listen. He pitied her.

"He said he loved me but didn't want a child. If I get rid of this child, he would love me again." She said to Earl. He did not know how to respond to that. All he knew was the anger welling up inside him, and it felt so overpowering he could not speak.

"Please don't tell Mrs. Johnson. She would be disappointed." Sarah begged him. "I'll take care of this somehow."

Earl agreed quietly, and he wanted to help Sarah.

Kevin did not return to the ranch to work the next day. Earl asked Mr. Johnson why he had not returned and then learned how much of a coward he truly was. Kevin quit; it was just the day after Sarah had told him she was pregnant. Sarah overheard their conversation and for week, she moped around the house. She believed she had lost her will to live. Sarah was depressed and Earl could not handle it. He tried to cheer her up to no avail.

The Johnsons were worried. She was out of it, losing weight and hardly ever leaving her room. Earl wished he had told them, but he felt compelled by his promise to Sarah to keep the truth a secret. One night, there was a scream from the room Sarah shared with Molly. Molly was a cherry little girl; she was barely twelve years old at the time. Earl and Neil rushed to the girls' room and found Sarah there. She was pale and grumbled to the ground. There was blood everywhere. None of it made any sense but luckily, the Johnsons had called an ambulance in time.

Earl began to doubt that keeping Sarah's secret was the right thing to do. She had tried to kill the baby, he thought but the bleach did more damage than she thought it would. The Johnsons were traumatized; he heard the revelation at the hospital that brought them to their knees. Earl could not tell for sure; he did not follow them to the hospital. He was convinced he was staying back to look out for Molly, but Duke knew him better than anyone- he was trying to escape from his guilt.

Mrs. Johnson was especially heartbroken; she felt like a mother's failure for not seeing the signs before it was too late. She blamed herself. '...maybe her negligence was why the Lord did not give her a child of her own, ' she thought as she crumbled and wailed bitterly. Her husband tried to console her; he felt he was equally to blame for their negligence. By the time they returned, they both looked like they had aged a decade overnight.

Earl was furious with himself. 'How could he have been so naive?' then, at his lowest, Duke came to him. Duke had not said a word in months; like a demon, he was waiting to pounce on Earl's insecurity for this very moment. Earl thought he was a horrible person but then he learned there was someone far worse than he was- Kevin.

"You were wrong... and now she's in pain. You've failed another person just like you failed your mother."

Duke made him shudder with tears and fury; like hook bait and sink, he had Earl where he wanted him. ***"Let's make it right... let's find the perve and end him."*** The thought dropped into his mind, shocking him. His body began to vibrate with the rush of adrenaline in his veins. He stormed out and ran to Kevin's house. By the time he got to the house he had seen Kevin walk into, he had calmed down a little. He knocked at the door and a woman heavily pregnant opened it.

"Hello, how can I help you?" She asked in a pleasant voice.

"I want to see Kevin," Earl said boldly, the anger he felt fueling his confidence.

"Oh, alright. Honey! There's a young man here to see you." She shouted, then turned and smiled at him. "He will be right out." She said, then noticed that his face had gone white.

"Are you alright?" She asked concerned. He did not speak but followed her when she gestured for him to follow her.

He followed her on wooden legs. The anger had left him, and he felt powerless and helpless. Instead, he sank into a chair the moment he could. Kevin came out of a room just then, saw Earl and quickly stepped towards him.

"What are you doing here? How did you find this place?" He asked, shaking Earl by the shoulders. He quickly shoved Earl out through the door, walking him to an alley.

"Sarah tried to have an abortion, and she's at the hospital now," Earl informed Kevin in a small voice. He already knew nothing could come out of this, not for him and definitely not for Sarah.

"So? How is that any of my business?" He asked nonchalantly. Earl thought he had experienced the height of emotions, but the statement Kevin made shocked him beyond imagination. He closed his eyes and opened them again.

Slowly, a pulsing '7' appeared on Kevin's forehead. Earl drew back, scared. He remembered seeing that same thing on his father and Duke's explanation for it. He quickly turned back and began to walk. "You're a bastard, and you don't deserve to live," he said, and Kevin pounced on him. Earl was stiff and yet Kevin could not strike him; it was not guilt that stopped him- it was fear.

He could see it in Earl's eyes. A blood lust so pure that for a moment, Kevin feared for his life and he let the boy walk away.

"If you ever come back here, I will kill you." Kevin's words to him as he vanished into the night.

He went home and waited. Earl was already mourning when the Johnsons returned and informed him of Sarah's passing. Mrs. Johnson tried to be strong but inevitably passed out from grief and shock. She was also hospitalized that day. Losing a child was not something to be taken likely, but losing a mother was just as bad.

Everything was falling apart.

"…And it's all your fault."

He should have known it would not last long.

"Fools do not deserve peace."

Why did I allow myself to become comfortable here?

"I did tell you not to." Duke's raspy voice said, having a mocking tone. ***"You only set yourself up for disappointment. Everyone would blame you for this. Do you think the Johnsons will keep you now? You watched that girl walk right into oblivion-."***

Earl began to count.

Maybe that's all he did, and he could not tell how long he counted for. He counted until Duke was gone, he counted until the pain was gone, he counted until his mind was gone and then he counted until Mrs. Johnson was gone. She never got better. Mrs. Johnson died in the hospital from a heart attack two days after. Her husband was devastated. Molly would not stop crying and Neil was angry. Earl felt nothing but guilt and believed it was his fault. He should not have kept Sarah's relationship with Kevin a secret nor even her pregnancy. The Johnsons would have found a way to stop all this from happening. There was no point crying over spilled milk, so Earl simply became mute.

He did not like the feeling of helplessness. He did not see the need for anything, especially taking his medication. Mrs. Johnson was dead, so there was no one to homeschool them anymore. Her husband was still grieving and noticed when he had let everything go. The man was barely even motivated to live. Earl went to town more often now. One of the boys he met in town introduced him to drugs. He tried them all in his desperate need to feel good and found that he preferred cocaine. The first time Earl had snorted the white powder, he had felt like he died and went to heaven. So he could have a few hours of reprieve from the hurt and anger he had been carrying for years. In fact, cocaine helped him to think more clearly- it helped Duke speak louder.

"You gotta be careful though. You don't wanna end up hooked on this shit." His 'friend' said before pushing him towards addiction.

"Don't worry about me, and I can control it." He said and just like that, using cocaine became an everyday routine.

He refused to touch alcohol though. He drew the line on anything alcoholic. He felt if he took a sip, he would become like his father. He wanted to run away from the Johnsons' home, but guilt did not allow him to. Earl was convinced he owed them; for once, there was nothing Duke could say to persuade him otherwise. He had found a better escape way than any medication or buzz liquor could grant him. He just needed to know how to pace his fixes.

Earl could not just leave Neil and Molly behind. He hated his sister for leaving him on the farm with his father, and he did not want them to hate him for leaving them behind too. He was going to stay put but would do everything on his own terms. Mr. Johnson enrolled them in school months later; he felt that was what his wife would have wanted. Earl kept to himself for the whole school year. He barely spoke to anyone and made no friends.

He only wanted to close his eyes and embrace an eternal slumber.

Then came Sophia and he felt like his world had light for once. She lit a fire in him, a fire that Duke used to consume him when she made the mistake of ridiculing him in front of the whole school. A fire that grew. It became large as Duke's dark hand wrapped around his heart, squeezing and squeezing until he could not feel anything else.

Only anger.

EARL WAS IN THE TWELFTH GRADE WHEN HIS MOTHER GOT out of jail. Miss. Horowitz came to find him in school, which was strange. It had been months since she checked on him and Earl was surprised that she would come to his school. Since the incident with Sophia, he had become a pariah at the school. Not like it was better before that. It was only worse now. "Hi. Earl." She greeted him with a smile when he stepped into the reception where she had been waiting for him.

"Hi." He responded without looking at her.

"Umm, there is someone who would like to meet you." She said, gesturing for him to follow her. They both walked out of the admin office towards the parking lot, and he wondered where she was taking him to.

"Your mom is here, Earl." She said, her smile becoming even larger. He stopped in his tracks and looked up sharply.

Was his mother here?

One… Two… Three… Four…

"…got out yesterday. Her sentence was lightened on the account that she suffered abuse from your father, and it was involuntary manslaughter. She can't wait…"

Earl had stopped listening. The roar in his ears drowned out Miss. Horowitz's words. His mother was directly in front of them, a few yards away. Contrary to what he had imagined, she had gained a bit of weight and looked as beautiful as ever. She had a bright smile on her face and her arms were opened wide for him. Tears poured down her face, causing her nose and eyes to be red. She was delighted to see him, but the feeling was not mutual.

The number was still on her.

"Hi, baby." She said through tears. She walked closer to where he was standing and slowly wrapped her arms around him. Earl stiffened and did not return the hug.

"She has the mark."

That was the thought running through his mind in a loop.

"The sin of wrath must be punished. We can't allow her to live, or it would fester and only hurt more than it needs to."

The fact that she was his mother and he loved her seemed inconsequential at that moment.

"I have explained the situation to the school, and you can take him with you for the rest of the day. What do you think, Earl?" Miss. Horowitz asked. Earl did not speak; he only nodded his head. Miss. Horowitz smiled at him and walked to her old, beat-up car, the same one she had driven him in that first time, and then she drove off. The silence that descended between Earl and his mother was palpable, and he was sure he could cut through it with a knife.

"Hmm…A knife. Sounds like you are subconsciously getting yourself ready for what we have to do."

…Five… Six… Seven… One…

He counted faster. He was not sure what would happen if he did not do that.

"Let's go, Earl. Let me buy you something cold. It's quite hot." Rose said, smiling at her son and leading him out of the school. Something was not quite right with him, and she had a feeling.

She shrugged her shoulders, dismissing the thought. Besides, who would not change having gone through what the boy had. She felt sorry for him and wanted to make things right with him. It might take a while, but she was going to prove to him that she was a better person, stronger than she had been before. She could protect him now. He still had not said a word to her. Rose did not ask but she wondered what he was thinking. She had thought he would have outgrown this awkwardness but apparently, he was still the same as he had been since he was little.

Rose remembered the incident that caused her son to become withdrawn. Her husband had been beating on her as usual and the poor kid of three years had come in between them. Tom had not cared if he killed the boy; he was blind drunk then. She bought them some ice cream and they sat down on a bench with umbrellas in what seemed like a park. The park was kind of empty and Rose was thankful for that. She wanted to talk to her son in a quiet place.

"How have you been, Earl?" She asked him, and he did not reply; neither did he raise his head. She was disappointed and did not know what to expect but had not expected the silent treatment.

"I know I haven't been the best mother but I'm here now, baby. Talk to me." She pleaded, stretching her hand across the table to touch him. Earl jerked backward, avoiding her touch.

"Don't touch me with your filthy hands, woman."

The voice and the look in his eyes startled Rose. She sat back quickly, drawing her hand back sharply.

"What is wrong with you, Earl? I am sorry and I am back to be better." She said, trying to reason with him. It wasn't that he did anything that should scare her but the look in his eyes. Even Tom had never looked at her with this much hatred. She had not been the best protector, but she knew she did not deserve this treatment from her son.

"I know you might still hate me for all you went through and for your sister leaving us, but we can be a family again." She said, her eyes pleading with him.

"I ALREADY HAVE A FAMILY."

Earl's voice was low and raspy. He could barely hear anything for the roar in his ears. His heart pounded and his hands were clammy with sweat.

"She has to go. We have to kill her." The voice in his head kept saying, over and over.

Earl blinked, sweat suddenly pouring down his face into his eyes. His breathing was labored, and he could barely control himself.

"I hate you!" He suddenly burst out. "I hate you so much!" He shouted again.

His mother looked around, thankful; no one was close enough to hear them.

"Earl, baby. I said I am sorry. I will do better henceforth." She said.

The fist around his heart squeezed tighter, causing him to feel as if his heart was going to burst. He suddenly stood up.

His mother sat back in fear, finally realizing her danger.

"Earl, calm down. I will leave if that is what you want. I love you and it would break my heart to leave you, but I will go if that is what you want." She said, tears dripping down her face.

Earl abruptly walked away from her, leaving her alone on the bench, his ice cream untouched and melted.

She watched as he walked further and further away.

"You spineless fool," Duke screamed in Earl's head. He quickly entered into an alley and held his head in his hands, and he could not do what Duke wanted him to do.

"I can't kill my mother." He whispered, tears pouring down his face.

"She has to go. You know how it is, and anyone with the mark is evil. And your mother has the mark."

One… Two…

Earl leaned against the wall and slid down to the ground until he was sitting on the ground. He did not mind that the alley was filthy.

"You have to do this."

"No, I don't. I can't."

"You have to do this."

…Three… Four… Five

"You have to do this."

"I have to do this."

…Six… Seven…

"You have to do this."

"I have to do this."

Earl rocked himself until the noise in his ears died down. He got up, deathly calm, and dusted his trousers. He was not himself but that did not matter. It was all like a trance. The alley he had walked into was not closed off and so led back to the school, through a grove of trees. The grove was between the park where he was seated. He walked through the grove and stood in the shadow of a tree from which he could see his mother there. Her back was turned to him, and she looked like she was crying.

He looked around him and picked up a heavy branch that had fallen. He held it in his hand, testing its weight. He nodded when he was satisfied that it would work. Earl looked around, making sure no one was around. When the coast was clear, he snuck up behind his mother and hit her on the head with the branch. She let a yelp but fell unconscious. He quickly dragged her back into the grove. He had no time to lose. When he was sure he was not visible, he laid his hands around her neck and tightened his grip. Slowly but surely choking her.

She began to struggle against him, but he had become stronger, working on the ranch. Besides, she may have gained weight but still did not weigh much. She struggled but Earl kept tightening his grip around her neck. Slowly, she stopped fighting and then she lay still. Tears were in her eyes as she stared back at him in sadness. The feeling of her life leaving her body was nostalgic. Earl felt like the world was at his feet and he could do anything he wanted. When she grew still, he stared long and hard at her face.

"Finish it," Duke demanded.

The place grew darker in his eyes, but Earl sat with the body, staring at it. At her.

He slowly got up, took out a chisel he had taken from the Johnsons and slashed his mother's face in a fit of blind rage, carving the number seven over it.

The Chosen had begun his assignment.

THE NEXT MORNING, THE WHOLE TOWN OF CREST HILL was abuzz with news of the dead woman found with the number 7 carved on her forehead.

The police had no leads and missing persons yielded no results either. She was a stranger, and no one knew who she was. The only thing the police could determine was that she had just gotten out of jail and been in town to see her son. The distraught boy was interviewed but nothing came out of it. He could not have done anything of the sort. Earl was too frail for such an act- but Duke was not.

The case became a cold case. Over time, it became a legend, people embellishing the facts as the days went by.

CHAPTER
SEVEN

Anita Heath woke up the next morning hoping for a break. She dressed and quickly got her daughter dressed and ready for the day care.

"Mom, are you going to pick me up early today?" Her daughter asked, looking up at her with those big brown eyes.

"Baby, mom is going to try her best. But you know I am out there trying to catch bad guys." She said, kneeling down so she could be on the same eye level as her daughter. She nodded, looking wise beyond her age. Her daughter had spent more time alone than with either of her parents.

That was one of the reasons Anita had moved to Crest Hill. She had thought it would give her a slower pace and time to take care of her daughter and she had until now.

She dropped her daughter off at the day care and headed straight to work. She met Pete in front of the precinct already waiting for her, and he had her cup of coffee from the Crest Hill diner and handed it to her.

"We got a call from the victim's mother this morning," Pete informed her after she had taken her first sip. Anita paused with the cup halfway to her mouth and had a bad feeling about this.

"What is it? What happened?" She asked Pete. She looked at him closely, noticing the circles around his eyes. Anita was willing to bet that he had not caught much sleep, and she was sure she looked the same. Thank God for caffeine.

"Miss. Hernandez said she got a package this morning. It was a zip lock bag containing all of Sophia's clothes and the ones she had been wearing the day she was killed. The package was dropped at her apartment this morning, and she saw no one. It had no postmark but a little paper inscribed with date and time of death." He said, gritting his teeth in anger.

The sick bastard.

It took a while for Anita to find her voice.

"She's safe?" She finally asked, already heading to the car, and Pete followed her and got into the driver's seat. She buckled up as Pete sped towards Weeping Willow Street. They got there in five minutes. Already a squad car was in front of the building. Anita was relieved that Pete had sent someone over to watch the woman.

"Good thinking, Pete." She said, nodding at him. He nodded back at her and they proceeded to walk into the building.

The policeman Pete had dispatched stood in front of apartment 3D, and Anita nodded at him and walked into the room. Miss. Hernandez was sitting in the same bean bag she had sat in the day before when they had come by. She seemed to have shriveled up more. She looked so small, and her face seemed to have acquired some more wrinkles.

Her eyes were red and swollen, tears still running down her cheeks. She raised her head when they walked in but did not budge. She was holding the plastic bag in her arm, holding it gently like she was carrying a child.

The policeman at the door walked in with them.

"Detective, Miss. Hernandez would not relinquish the bag, and she did not let us take it from her." He informed Anita.

She nodded and walked toward the woman.

"Miss. Hernandez?" She called, gently approaching her. The woman looked at her, but Anita was sure she was not seeing her.

"He sent me my baby's clothes." She said in a broken voice. Anita closed her eyes, knowing how she felt, having lost a loved one.

"Shit!" She heard Pete mutter behind her. She turned and looked at him; he looked like he could punch the wall in anger, and she felt the same.

"I know exactly how you feel, Miss. Hernandez. But you know we need everything we can get to catch the sick bastard." Anita said, crouching so she could look into the woman's eyes.

"We will catch him, I promise you." She promised. The woman looked down at the bag she was holding and slowly handed it to Anita.

"I have not opened it at all, and I could not bring myself to do that." She informed Anita, who quickly handed it over to the policeman, and he in turn took it to the precinct.

"Did you see anyone?" Anita asked Miss. Hernandez.

"No, I did not. There was a knock at my door very early in the morning but no one was there by the time I got there. I looked down and saw the package. At first, I thought there must have been a mistake until I looked closely at it, and there was a piece of paper with my name on it." Miss. Hernandez continued.

Anita listened carefully while Pete took notes.

"Alright, Miss. Hernandez. You be careful and do not open the door to anyone. We will keep a policeman to watch over you if you do not mind." She responded. The woman seemed to have spaced out and did not respond. After a few minutes of looking around, Anita and Pete excused themselves.

"Let us take a walk around the neighborhood," Anita said to Pete. She wanted to know all the possible routes one could take and where they led to. "This person must be a local, and seeing as he knows how to move about the neighborhood easily."

They walked around the neighborhood, mapping streets and noting how they connected to each other. The apartment on Weeping Willow was just a block from the grocery store, two blocks from the grove of trees.

"I believe our perp must have watched the building, keeping track of Sophia's movements," Anita said. They stood in front of the building and looked around, trying to find a spot suitable for someone to watch the building from.

"What is that place? The one with the small side window?" She asked, noticing a store directly across the apartment building. Anita crossed the street and entered the store. A tinkling sound came when she opened the door.

"Hi there. Come in and make yourself comfortable." Mrs. Golding, the owner of the shop, said when they walked in. It was a bookstore that doubled as a library. The elderly woman behind the counter looked like she was at least eighty.

"Hello, Ma'am." Anita said, approaching the counter.

"Yes, dear. Do you want to borrow a book or buy one?" The woman asked, squinting at Anita and Pete. She had a pair of glasses hung around her neck but was not wearing them. Anita bet the woman could not see anything beyond her nose. Her eyes were rheumy and looked glazed over with cataract.

Anita realized the need for the tinkles with the door, and that was probably the only way this woman knew someone had entered her store.

How come she had not been robbed blind? Anita chuckled under her breath realizing the pun in her thoughts. Then she sighed. This woman couldn't have seen anything.

"I am Anita Heath, and this is my partner Pete Morales from the Police department. We would like to ask you a few questions about what you may have seen on the day of the murder." Anita said.

"Did you say, Pete Morales? Hey, Petey, boy! How are you doing? How is your momma doing? She ain't been to my store in a while." The woman said, smiling broadly at them. Anita looked back at Pete who looked embarrassed.

"Hey, Mrs. Golding. I am well, thank you. My momma's doing great, but she lives on the ranch these days. Bad hip." He replied.

Anita shook her head, gesturing for him to take over.

"Hey, Mrs. Golding. Could you perhaps recall anything strange that might have happened three days ago at your store, ma'am? Did any strange person come in that day?" He asked.

The woman looked thoughtful for a while then shook her head.

"Nothing stands out in this old brain of mine." She said with a self-deprecating chuckle.

"Do you happen to have cameras installed in your store?" Anita asked.

"Cameras! Ha! No one dares to steal nothing' from this here store. I got sharp senses, so no need for cameras." The woman said with pride, looking insulted that Anita would suggest that she could not handle her store and needed electronic help.

Anita walked around the store, taking note of different vantage points. She noticed a window in the far corner of the store with a comfortable-looking couch, and she went to the corner and sat on the couch.

"Hmmmm," Anita said, looking around. Perfect view of the apartment building opposite and the whole store, and she could see everything yet not be seen. Pete followed her and saw what she was doing.

Anita stood up, took one more look around, and then walked out of the store, Pete on her heels.

"Thank you, Mrs. Golding," Pete said before exiting the store. The old woman nodded and gave an almost toothless smile.

"Tell your momma to come to see me sometime, Petey." She called after him.

"Yes, ma'am," Pete said as they walked out.

"Officer Petey, I think Mrs. Golding still thinks of you as a middle schooler," Anita said to Pete, smiling when his face grew red.

"Yes, she does. My friends and I used to hang out here when I was in middle school." He chuckled as they kept walking.

All the streets looked similar and connected in one way or another. Anita could see how the perp could walk around the neighborhood easily without raising suspicion.

"He must have easily blended in. I am of the opinion that he watched Sophia from Mrs. Golding's bookstore from that couch I sat on earlier. I could see everything happening across the street from that place without being seen or disturbed." Anita said to Pete.

Pete nodded, seeing what she meant. The killer knew the area very well, at least enough to easily move from place to place within the neighborhood without being detected or suspected. It meant that he knew his way around and could easily blend in.

"Maybe, even someone everybody knows," Pete said, the thought unsettling him.

EARL SAT AT HIS DESK AT THE BMV, UNABLE TO DO ANY work. He was elated and was rather proud of himself this morning. All his previous restraints were gone, and now he understood entirely why Duke enjoyed what he did. He could only imagine the uproar in the precinct. They would be furious and baffled at the same time. He could give anything to be able to see the detective's face right now, he thought. His face was stretched in a wide grin that Bertha was worried about him. She had never seen him make such a face. She had asked him three times if he was alright.

It was a stroke of genius, he thought, the idea to send the woman her daughter's clothes. He could not keep them any longer. He no longer needed them. Burning them would raise suspicions. Throwing them in the trash would have been too mundane. Nothing exciting about mundane. Sending them to her mother on the other hand? That was a brilliant idea. He had kept something for himself though. He could not just give up everything. Earl reached into his pants pocket, grabbing the little black scrap of material she had been wearing around her crotch. The thought of where it had been excited him to the point that Earl could barely sit still.

"You better watch it. Do not raise suspicions."

He tried to compose himself for the rest of the day. Funny, Duke was suddenly his voice of reason. 'How the tables have turned.'

"Hey, Earl?" Jim, his supervisor called poking his head into Earl's office.

"Yes, Mr. Harris," Earl answered, raising his head.

"Can I see you in my office? Before you leave?" He asked. Earl looked at his wristwatch, and he was due to clock out in fifteen minutes and would have preferred not to wait a minute longer.

He still had an errand to run this night, but he had never said no to his boss before. Doing so now would only raise suspicions, which he did not need.

"Alright, Boss." He replied with a smile. The man smiled back on his way out.

"I will not take much of your time, and I only have a few questions to ask you." He said before leaving.

What could he want to ask? Earl thought. He had not felt like coming to work these past three days since he had a bigger and more important assignment now. But he had decided to keep coming. So, Jim would not question him about his absence from work.

"Why does Jim want to see you?" His nosy colleague, Bertha, enquired. Sometimes, it was all he could do not to strangle the woman. He plastered a smile, this one noticeably different from the one he had on earlier and shrugged. Whatever it was, Earl did not care. He mentally shrugged his shoulders and continued to read through the document he was working on. When he was done with work, Earl packed up his things and got ready to leave. He stopped by Jim's office, knocking on the door.

"Come in!" He heard Jim call from inside and opened the door.

"Hey, Mr. Harris. You wanted to see me?" Earl said as he walked into Jim's office.

"Yes, Earl. Please come in and have a seat." The man said, standing up from behind his desk and walking to the sofa on the other side of the room. He gestured for Earl to sit in the one-seater while he sat on the sofa, a small coffee table between them.

Earl sat at the edge of the seat, not liking this one bit.

"So, Earl. How have you been?" Jim asked him. Looking at Earl's face intently. What was this man trying to do? Earl thought.

"I am doing very fine, Mr. Harris." He said, trying to keep the conversation short.

"Are you really?" Jim asked. Earl hated when people talked down to him like they were talking to a child. Jim was old enough to be his father, but Earl was old enough to know if he was fine or not.

Where was this conversation going?

"Yes, really, sir." He replied, allowing a smile. The man smiled back but Earl sensed a hint of sadness or was that disappointment he sensed?

"I believe you if you say so. But I have noticed some things with your work lately that were not there before." Jim said, standing up to get a folder he had kept on his desk. He spread the forms and documents out on the coffee table, and Earl could see that they were documents he had filled in from his handwriting.

"Your work has been sloppy these days, Earl. Now, I know you better than this. You take your work seriously, and which was why I was surprised when I noticed these lapses." Jim said.

Earl almost chuckled when the man had said he knew him. Instead, he picked up the documents and raised them to his face to hide his smile. He looked at them and noticed the mistakes he had made. He had approved a license for a young lady who had failed her driving test and had disapproved one for a woman with perfect results and qualifications, among other mistakes. He felt a tinge of guilt, almost like reality had dawned on him, but only for a moment.

"The most baffling mistakes I saw were the scribbles you added to a form," Jim said, rummaging through a sheaf of papers to find the said form. When he found it, he handed it to Earl who looked at it and for the first time, felt truly alarmed. He had absentmindedly scribbled the number 7 over the applicant's picture. He remembered the young lady well. She had come in with an attitude that had annoyed Earl just the day before. He had wondered if only she knew who it was that was attending to her; she probably would bring that attitude down a notch. His heart began to pound, and he felt like a deer in headlights.

One… Two… Three… Four…

He began to count to calm himself down.

This is bad. If Jim ties it with the detail from the murder…

Five… Six… Seven…

"Oh. I am sorry, Mr. Harris. I've had a lot on my mind lately." He said, looking at his boss, trying to make himself look preoccupied and worried.

"What is the matter, Earl?" Jim asked, concerned.

"I used to know the woman who was murdered," Earl answered earnestly. "And you can imagine how our peaceful Crest Hill has been thrown into turmoil. I have just been worried." He finished, putting his hand on his temples in a look of worry, hoping that Jim would believe him.

"I know what you mean, Earl. We have all been worried, and I am scared to allow my daughter to leave the house these days. You know you can talk to me and if you need a few days off, you can always take them. Maybe go back to Milk Ranch for a few days? You deserve some time off." The man said, looking at him with concern.

"I will consider that, Mr. Harris. Thank you for your concern and understanding." Earl said as he stood up. Jim quickly stood with him and led him out the door.

Earl walked out of the office with his head held high, but he was barely keeping himself from exploding. He looked around to see if anyone was watching and walked into the alley one block away from the BMV.

"One… Two… Three." He counted, kicking the trash can as he counted, pausing when he got to the number seven.

"How could you be so stupid?" Duke's rasping voice filled his head. "I thought I could trust you to do everything by yourself only for you to mess up!"

"I'm sorry. I'm so sorry." Earl said, leaning on the wall and sliding down until he was sitting on the ground. He had begun to sob, his head between his raised knees. "I'm not used to all this yet."

"That was a close call. We need to be more careful, and these small lapses could be dangerous for us." Duke said, his voice softer. The softest it had ever been.

"I won't let this happen again. We'll be fine." He swore.

"Now get up, clean yourself up. We have an errand to run." He commanded.

Earl stood to his feet and wiped his face on his shirt sleeve. He smoothed his rumpled shirt with his hand, hitched his small office bag higher on his shoulder and walked out of the alley, composed. Looking at him, no one would be able to tell that he had just had a mental breakdown. Or that he was a psychopath capable of murder.

To make matters worse… Duke was back in charge.

THE WINDOW BUDGED EASILY AFTER EARL SHOOK THE lock. He was so excited that he needed to stop and take a deep breath before going into the house. He had missed seeing Ciara that night, but this would make it all worth it. He had to do this. He entered the apartment quietly, careful not to make any sounds in case she had any pets around. Apparently, she was not an animal person.

After making sure that he was alone, Earl moved from room to room like he owned the place, although it was still dark. He could not put on any lights. He did not want anyone to suspect that Ciara's place had been broken into. Well, not really broken into. He was not a stranger to Ciara. In fact, they had become close friends over the past weeks and Earl was even ready to take it to the next step. Maybe even marry her. He chuckled with delight at the thought. He took a deep breath. The room smelt of summer. She had a few pots of flowers on the window in her kitchen. The kitchen looked like she used it often. Good, she liked home-cooked meals too. A perfect match made in heaven, Earl thought.

Her living room looked perfect too, although he would have loved it if some things were arranged differently. Ciara hung various picture frames on the wall of her family members brond friends. There was one where she was dressed in a cap and gown and holding a diploma. She was with Tonya Howell at what looked like a club in another picture frame. A man he did not recognize had his arm around her. Earl grimaced at it; none of it sat well with him.

He turned away from the pictures, and they were not his objective. He walked into her bedroom. It was exactly as he had imagined it was going to be. He could not see the colors clearly but imagined she had some soft pinks and purples. The only light was from a streetlight outside coming in through the window. He walked around the room careful not to trip on anything or move anything. He took pictures of the room and looked through her drawers. On the countertop beside her bed, Ciara had left her diary. Earl was elated. He could take a peek into her personal thoughts and feelings. Maybe she had even written about him in her diary.

Earl went through the small book then carefully replaced it. He continued to look around the room. He looked in her closet and found it neatly arranged. He walked into the small closet, held one of her clothes to his nose and took a deep breath. 'Ahhhh…' He moaned loudly as Ciara's scent filled his nose. He became ecstatic, so much so that he was convinced he could feel himself wrapped in her embrace. It was intoxicating to him. Earl decided that he was going to keep at least one of her clothing items with him. He carefully rifled through her drawers and came up with a red thong.

Nothing better than a piece of cloth that has been in contact with her most private parts. He chuckled as he stuffed it into his pocket. Her queen-size bed was neatly made, edges folded neatly. He liked neat. Earl had grown up in a filthy environment, so he had developed a thing for putting things in their place and making sure everything was neatly arranged. Everything had its place in Ciara's apartment, just as he liked things to be like he said.

A match made in heaven.

Earl let himself out of the apartment through the same way he had come in. His work was finished for the night, and he was going to sleep, dreaming of Ciara. The love of his life.

Anita Heath stood in the office of the lead Crime scene investigator, waiting for the results on the clothing the killer had sent to the victim's mother. Logan Miller looked at the document on his desk. He could recite everything he had written in it without looking at it but opted to read it out so he would not miss anything.

"The clothing items he had brought had been washed with a common detergent. We could not trace any scent or fluid on them that would give us a clue to who this killer was." He explained to Detective Heath.

"We also examined the clothing for any other chemicals and even tested to see want kind of water was used. We could not trace anything specific enough to give you a direction, and everything he used is common to everyone or most people in Crest Hill." Logan finished.

Logan had been on the job for a long time now but had yet to see a killer take his victims so personally.

"Why do you think he washed them before sending them to the mother?" He asked Anita.

She shook her head, already exasperated.

"Who knows? Maybe because he's a sick bastard or because he didn't want anything on the clothes to be traced to him?" She said, looking frustrated.

"Any item of clothing missing?" She asked.

"Well, I noticed that there was everything a woman should be wearing here except panties. But then, she probably was not wearing them when he took her." He replied. Underwear.

"He's keeping trophies, and I am almost a hundred percent sure of that." She informed Logan, who looked horrified. He thought he had seen it all, but people would always surprise you with how demented and evil their actions could be.

"How about the note he left?" Anita asked. Logan and his team had examined the paper and the ink for any peculiarities that would make identifying the killer easy.

"Unfortunately, it is the same with the note. I even had a psychologist friend of mine examine the handwriting; all he could come up with was what you already concluded. This person is very meticulous and may be suffering from some mental disorder. From the note, I can see that he thinks he is doing the world a favor." Logan said. Anita nodded and stood to her feet.

"Thank you for your time, Logan. Please reach out to me if anything new comes up." Anita said, shaking his hand before leaving the office.

She drove to the precinct, her mind preoccupied with the case. They needed a break soon. Or she feared this was only going to get darker.

CHAPTER
EIGHT

Earl looked at the young woman sitting across from him at the Bureau of Motor Vehicles. Already, the day had been long and boring, and now he had to deal with a spoilt brat with a smart mouth. Looking at her, Earl could feel his blood boil. He thought a few minutes alone with her would teach her to mind her manners.

"You could get more than a few minutes with her, you know."

As he looked down at her license application form, the thought flashed through his mind. Her address was written in bold letters. He looked up at her and smiled.

"Ma'am, your application will be examined, and the results of your tests will be collated. You can return for your license in four working days." He said to her.

"But this is the weekend! I have to wait four whole days to get my license?" She shouted like a spoilt brat.

Earl gritted his teeth and put his hands under his desk to keep from hitting her. The number seven had appeared on it, and he became restless and quickly stood up.

"Someone has to give me my license right now and I don't give a fuck what has to happen for me to have it. I need to see your supervisor." She said at the top of her voice. Bertha, whose desk was beside Earl's and had been attending to someone else was dumbfounded. Earl looked down at her application form again.

Julia Alvarez*.*

The girl gave him an annoyed look, and Earl looked back at her with the same amount of annoyance. She looked like one of those spoilt brats that seemed to have the world at their fingertips.

"How hard could it be to operate a computer?" She asked him loudly, not caring that she was not the only person in the BMV.

"Ma'am, it's a standard procedure for us. You have to come back after four working days to pick up your license, and your license would be ready by then as long as you are qualified." Earl replied, barely keeping his composure.

"I don't give a fuck what your standard procedures are, and I want my license now. You only have to push a button here and there to find my records." She said out loud, her voice becoming louder. She ran her painted nails through her long black hair impatiently. She had just added blonde streaks to the hair and thought she looked good.

"You know what we have to do."

Her black hair with blonde streaks was matted with the blood as the wound on her forehead bled. At first, the blood had not been there but then it appeared when she started to shout, calling attention to herself and him. He had immediately clenched his hands under the desk, trying very hard not to hit her in the face. Anytime he saw that mark, he knew. He just knew they were evil. He had to do something about them. He had to rid the world of the evil who had been sitting in front of him.

Jim Harris must have heard her shouting because he came out of his office.

"Calm down ma'am. How can I help you?" He asked—finally, someone important who would listen to her.

"This weirdo wouldn't give me my license. I paid my dues, took my tests and everything. He is just like, discriminating against me." She told the man.

"Come with me, please," Jim said, leading her to his office after taking her file from Earl. Earl knew he was not going to tell her anything different. He just wanted to diffuse the scene she was causing. Julia looked at Earl with a condescending look. The look on his face caused a chill to run through her body. She inhaled sharply at the hatred she saw in his eyes. She had never met him before and wondered why he would hate her. Everybody loved her. She mentally shrugged her shoulders and followed the other man to his office. She stomped out of that office a few minutes later. The boss had refused to give her a license either. She hissed and walked out. A call came in from her boyfriend and she proceeded to narrate all that had happened, both real and imagined to him before finally walking out of the Bureau of Motor Vehicles.

Earl sat at his desk and watched as the girl sashayed out of the exit door.

"She's one of them." He heard Duke whisper to him as the girl walked out of the office.

"You know what we have to do." Duke nagged and Earl nodded. He was glad he had taken note of her home address. He could barely concentrate on the rest of the work he had for the day but managed to finish it up. He knew exactly what needed to be done.

EARL STOOD ACROSS THE ROAD FROM THE GIRL'S APARTMENT building. The building was in the highbrow area of Crest Hill. This meant that Earl had to dress in a way that fit into the environment. This evening, he was dressed like a middle-aged man living in the suburbs. A part of him liked the disguises; it gave him an excuse to try out the clothes he normally would never have thrown on. Earl had stopped by the diner both to see Ciara and create an alibi for himself. After having dinner, he complained of a headache and said he was going to sleep. He called Bertha to inform her that he was not feeling well, and she had promised to bring him soup the next morning.

He had even called Mr. Johnson. Two calls in one week, the man must have been surprised but pleasantly so from the tone of his voice when they had talked.

"Getting her won't be so easy." Duke insisted and it irritated him. Easy, difficult- none of that matter. Earl was just eager to make her disappear. He did not take long to plan this one, but he could think on his feet. He had a creative mind and was impulsive. He held his nose between his thumb and forefinger and sniffed loudly. He had just snorted some cocaine and wanted to sniff up any residue in his nose. He wiped his nose with his palm and rubbed his hands together. He felt his body thrumming with anticipation. He could not afford the time needed to watch her. He needed to act quickly. He had the whole weekend to himself and could do whatever he wanted.

Just then, the 'witch' he was after walked out of the apartment building dressed in a short red dress and a pair of black heels that looked like stilts. It was almost like she had been served on a platter of gold for him. She wore a light jacket over the dress. Her hair had been pulled into a bun and she wore large hoop earrings. She looked fancy like she had prepared for him. She may look good, but that ugly mark was still on her forehead.

"Turns out we don't need to wait so long." Duke commended. Earl could feel the excitement course through his body. The blood rushing through his veins and his heartbeat sped up. He rubbed his hands together before putting them into his jacket pockets. He felt the pointed end of his chisel and ran his index finger over it. He stood at the street corner, watching her tap her foot impatiently on the sidewalk. She must be waiting for someone. He would wait for a while, allowing her to meet whomever she wanted to meet. He had thought a lot about how to deal with this evil. An ordinary strangling would not do. He was not short of ideas, but he needed one fitting for this particular case of self-absorption.

"Don't forget, you were born to do this special task. That was why no one ever understood you." Duke told him, causing Earl to feel more confident. He followed the girl with purposeful strides, knowing he was doing the world a favor. He was not going to let what happened to his mother repeat itself. The more he let these evils be the more people they infected. Evil spreads like a nasty disease. It was his destiny to stop it from spreading. Julia waited on the street for Darren. He was supposed to pick her up. She was already getting impatient. After a lousy day, things had just begun to look better. She was meeting up with her boyfriend, Darren. They had been dating for barely two months, and he was taking her shopping tonight. She needed to buy a few clothes and shoes to make this day get better. Forget that she had so many clothes that she did not know what to do.

Julia had carefully chosen her clothes, making sure that she would be the only one catching any attention at the restaurant and then the boutique. Everyone had to know she was around and do everything for her. A few minutes later, Darren pulled up in his Honda. Julia had become so angry she could spit in his face.

"How dare you keep me standing on the street for this long? I have been waiting for you." She exploded immediately after he stepped out of the car.

"Hey, babe!" He said, pretending he did not hear her.

"Don't "hey babe!" me, Darren. You know I could have my own car and not have to let you put me through this shit. You should do everything for me not make me stress out like this." She said and promptly burst into tears.

Darren walked round the car and held her in his arms.

"I am sorry babe; I was just a minute late." He said, wrapping his arms around her. She sniffed and pulled out of his embrace.

"You don't ever do what I want. You don't think about me, Darren. I don't deserve this." She said and stomped into the car. Darren sighed and walked to the driver's side of the car and got in.

"I am sorry babe. It won't happen again." He said as he pulled into the road.

"It had better not. Or you will be hearing from my daddy's lawyers." She said with a pout.

"Alright, babe." Darren knew how liquid her emotions could be, so he just agreed with whatever she said. He wondered what he was doing with a girl as self-absorbed as Julia. Then he remembered. The sex was good, he thought, chuckling to himself.

They were both as toxic as they were marked.

The restaurant was a few blocks from Julia's apartment, yet she had insisted that he come to pick her up in his car. At the restaurant, she made a fuss about the seat arrangement. She said the seats were too much to the back and wanted them to be moved to the front close to the live band where they could get all the attention. He just wanted to eat, take her shopping and then go back home for sex, and then he would return home accomplished. Dinner was beautiful but Darren could barely enjoy it for her nagging. They left the restaurant after an hour but not before Julia had all the staff on their toes for not taking care of her needs. They arrived at the boutique, where Julia had everyone in the store waiting on her. By the time they had left, all the staff at the boutique were already exhausted.

"Darren, how dare you?!" She asked when they got into his car after buying all that she wanted. He paused wracking his brain about what he could have done or not done for her this time?

"What babe?" He asked, ready to apologize for whatever was real or imagined.

"I saw you were staring at that girl at the store and totally checking her out." She said, her voice already getting hysterical.

"What girl? What do you mean I was checking her out?" He asked, not remembering any girl. Besides, he had been looking through his phone the whole time she was shopping and had not checked any girls out. He tried to tell her this, but she just became more hysterical. There goes his plan for the night. He wasn't getting any tonight. Darren thought that he had lost his appetite even if she calmed down.

Darren dropped her off at the front of her apartment building later that night and drove off before she had the opportunity to slam the door. She stomped into the building and into the first-floor apartment, banging on everything. A little while later, a knock sounded on her door.

"I knew he was going to come back to apologize." She said, allowing the knock to continue for a while before walking to the door. She held the doorknob but did not open it.

"Darren, you can save your apology, and I do not want to hear it." She said through the closed door. There was silence on the other side.

Will he not apologize? Wasn't that what he had come back to do? So, he was going to be like this? She humped and opened the door. Immediately she did, the person pushed the door open and walked in. Julia backed up against the wall opposite the door. A man wearing a janitorial uniform stood in front of her; his gloved hand was around her neck quicker than she could blink.

"Darren?" She asked, her voice becoming panicked.

"Not Darren. In fact, Darren will be glad to be finally rid of you." The man said in a low and raspy voice.

"Who are you?" She asked

"I am Redemption." He said before landing a blow to her temple with the hammer he had wrapped in clothes prior, knocking her unconscious.

I am Redemption

Earl chuckled, remembering how he had spoken before knocking Julia unconscious. He had sounded so cool. The easiest way for him to have entered the apartment building was to be dressed as a janitor. He had accessed the janitor's closet, borrowed a uniform, then picked up a trash can and went to Apartment 1B. He had been worried that they would find it strange that the janitor was going round the apartments at that time but apparently, no one cared. No one had batted an eyelash at him. The rich and their ways, he thought shaking his head.

Getting her out of the complex in the trash can had been fairly easy. He had parked his car a few blocks away. Knowing his way around alleys and backroads had been helpful. Having her weigh next to nothing was also good. In fifteen minutes, he had driven away with Julia in his trunk. The drive was not long. Only about thirty minutes. He had decided to use a more familiar place this time. It was far enough out of town to be hidden but close enough for him to commute from there to the main town. He arrived at his old family ranch and parked in front of the old house. It had been falling apart all those years ago but now, it was overgrown with weeds.

He killed the engine but remained in the car. It was dark, so he could not see but looked directly at where he knew the old house would be. He had not been to the house in a long while. Almost fifteen years to the day. He had not returned to this place since he and his mother had been taken away by the police that day.

A thumping sound came from the trunk. Julia was awake. Time to get to work, he thought smugly. He got down from the car, went to the trunk and opened it.

"Mmh! Mph! Mmm!" She grunted desperately trying to talk through the dirty rag he had gagged her with. He tied her hands and feet behind her, so she lay in a reverse fetal position. He roughly removed the gag he had placed in her mouth knowing that even if she screamed, no one would hear her out here. No one had heard his mother's screams all those years when they had both been battered by his father. Earl lifted Julia out of the trunk and roughly carried her towards the large oak tree that used to be his hideout. He had not put on any lights, yet he could still find his way to the tree in the dark. It was almost like he had a homing beacon that could pick the tree's location in the dark even after many years.

"Put me down. What do you think you are doing?" Julia was screaming, pounding his back. For all her pounding, it felt like being caressed with a feather. Reaching the tree, he dropped her roughly to the ground. He was not worried she would run. Even if she managed to be free of the cords with which he had tied her with, there was nowhere for her to run to. The town was a long way off on foot. He tied her to the tree, still not needing any lights, using his customary seven knots. She struggled a lot, which made tying her up a little hard, but he managed it.

"No one ever gets away with laying hands on me. My daddy is going to find you and you will surely rot in jail." She said to him. Her nagging was annoying him to no end, so he just gagged her again.

"Mmm… mmm," she mumbled through the gag still trying to talk. He stripped her of her light nightwear, exposing her body. She shivered as the cold night air made contact with her skin. Her skin puckered up and her small, pink nipples stood out against the white of her skin in the cold.

He looked at her body briefly but felt nothing. He could admit that she was lovely though. If he were evil, then maybe he would have had his way with her. "Will you shut the fuck up?" He yelled at her, roughly removing the gag from her mouth. The volume of his voice finally achieved what he wanted. She became silent. She had probably realized what she was in for. She began to sob, tears and snot rolling down her face. Earl wondered how they all seemed to cry and were never pretty when they cried.

"What… what do you want? My daddy will give you anything you want. Just let me go. I did not see your face and can't tell the police anything. Please just let me go." She blubbered.

"Your father has nothing I want or need. You have to learn a lesson, and the world does not revolve around you." He said with a quiet voice. She was listening, for once.

"You have been given so much as a privilege, but you have taken it all as a right, not minding who else goes without. You are rude, spoilt and without any inhibitions." Earl said. The anger and hatred he felt pouring out in his voice as he spoke. The hatred she was hearing seemed to shock her more than the words he was speaking.

"But I have not ever done anything to you. I don't even know you." She said, looking incredulous.

Earl chuckled, removed his cap, and drew his hoodie down.

"I don't know you... wait. You are the guy from the BMV. What did I do that was so wrong?" She asked him, recognition filling her face.

"If she still doesn't know, then she is irredeemable."

"There's no point telling you. It won't matter anyway," he said crouching until his face was on the same level as hers. He looked into her face, seeing nothing but fear and greed in them to contrast the glee in his. He took out his chisel and marked her, relishing the blood pouring down her forehead unto her face and her clothes. She struggled, crying out loud as the chisel dug into her skull. She did not pass out but was conscious throughout. He preferred this to her passing out. He thought that if she passed out, she would not feel the pain and would not learn her lesson. By the time he had finished, she was sobbing so loud trying to talk but her words were unintelligible. Earl did not care. She had nothing of interest to say to him.

"I hope you have learned your lesson now." He said to her. She nodded her head vigorously, hoping to creep into her eyes. She looked like she thought he was going to release her. He liked the feeling of power he had, knowing the truth was about to dawn on her. By then, it would have been too late. He allowed her to rest for a bit, even going as far as giving her a drink of water which she drank thirstily. He admonished her while she drank and for once, probably in her entire life, she was listening to someone else talk. When she had drunk to her fill, Earl went to the car and brought out a small pillow from the trunk. He had thought of bashing her head in but then carving the number on her head would have been for nothing. Then he thought of slitting her throat, but he feared that he would have gotten more blood than he needed all over him, so He had brought the girl's pillow along with him, having decided the best way to finish her up. He went behind her, at the other end of the tree and with his gloved hands, placed the pillow over her face and gradually applied pressure. He only wanted her to be unconscious. This was not the way she had to die. The girl thrashed around, making it difficult to cut off her air supply effectively.

The best way to finish this was to ensure she could never be rude to anyone again. Take away her ability to talk. He had come prepared. He brought out the bottle of hydrochloric acid he had stashed in there just as he was leaving home that evening. He went around the tree to stand in front of her and gently poured the whole bottle down her throat. She gagged and thrashed but soon enough, and Earl began to perceive the smell of burning flesh as the acid broke down the proteins in her throat and then her stomach. A little gurgling sound was all she made, and Earl could see the life drain out of her. A dribble of saliva and blood ran down the side of her mouth and he gently cleaned it with a wipe. He knew he was doing a good thing, but the world was still blind to people like her. Only he knew what good he was doing for humanity, especially those he loved. The woman he loved.

He still had enough time to stash her body where the world would easily see her. He had brought along a large plastic bag with which he wrapped her body and stuffed it in his trunk, making sure there could be no trace of her left in the car once he lifted her out. He burnt the pillow and her clothes in the old incinerator his family had used while they had lived there before leaving. However, he kept her blue panties.

"One more for our collection." Duke cheered.

He was done playing games now.

"It is going to be strictly business from here on out."

THE NEXT MORNING, ANITA AND PETE WERE AT ANOTHER site where another woman had been found dead, her body stripped of clothes. The same mark on her forehead, but she had been killed much more agonisingly this time. The stench of burnt flesh could be perceived even from more than ten feet away. It looked like he had killed the girl by pouring acid down her throat. Anita looked around the dump site, trying to fathom the significance of this location; the woman had been dumped at the intersection between the mayor's residence and the police precinct.

"A way of mocking the government, perhaps?" Pete asked, having noticed the location. They already knew that their killer did not do anything without reason. Anita shrugged, already tired of the case. Anger and a sense of duty to the people of Crest Hill were all that kept her going. She had brought her daughter to this town in order to give her a more peaceful childhood and did not care a bit for this.

"This guy is getting sicker by the day. Have you been able to uncover any unsolved cases with similar M.O. as this one?" Anita asked Pete. The killer's note had made reference to another murder, and she wanted to see if there was ever a case like that among the cold cases.

"I am still looking through the old case files. You will know as soon as I find something." Pete said, looking through his computer for the file.

Anita nodded.

"Look on the body. I am sure he must have left a note again. He must be enjoying himself, watching us bum around without any real clue." She said, looking around the area. It was still quite early, and the streets were still quiet. A few early risers had noticed the commotion and were watching from safe distances. The person who saw the body and reported it to the police was an old truck driver. He said he had been on his way to the truck yard when he had encountered the dead woman and immediately called 911.

Pete approached the dead woman. The body had been covered up with a sheet while the crime scene people went around looking for traces of the killer and other clues. He reached for the edge of the sheet, lifting it slightly. There was no note between the woman's fingers but looking at her face, and her mouth looked like it had been forced shut with some kind of glue. It was not the strong kind but enough to make Pete struggle a bit to open her mouth. Pete carefully pried it open and to his disgust, there was a small piece of paper between her lips. He gently pried it out with a pair of tweezers. Anita had reached him by this time, seeing that he had crouched and looked like he had found something.

"Found something?" She asked, hoping this would give them a break they had been looking for. Pete solemnly nodded his head, turning to show her the piece of paper. As expected, he had left them a note.

BEFORE YOU LAY THE THIRD- JULIA ALVAREZ – GREED AND SELF ABSORPTION.

SHE DESERVED TO DIE. ANOTHER EVIL OUT OF THE WORLD.

"Send it to the lab and have Logan look at it thoroughly. Hopefully, he would have made a mistake this time." Anita said to Pete who put the paper in a zip lock bag and handed it to one of the crime scene techs.

"At least, he has saved us time by identifying the victim for us," Pete said, going into his squad car to call in the clue. He asked the operator at the other end to search for and send records for a Julia Alvarez, a woman in her mid to late twenties. Within twenty minutes, a report had been sent back to him via email with the woman's full identity. Pete opened the file and immediately whistled.

"You may have been right about his motive, Detective. Look who her father is." He said, showing Anita the report that had been sent to him.

"Woah… Her father is the senior adviser to the mayor's office. Julio Alvarez. I knew the name sounded familiar." Anita said turning to the crime scene people.

"We need to pack this up as soon as possible. This case has just taken a more unexpected turn. Let us see if we can leave this place with the body and all evidence in about thirty minutes." She instructed them. Everyone dispersed to do their jobs.

Once the press gets a hold of the victim's identity, all hell would break loose, making it harder to carry out their investigations in peace.

"Place a call to the senior adviser's office. We need to inform the father of his daughter's demise as soon as possible." Anita instructed. Pete's phone rang just then.

"I think I may have found something. I will email you the files." He said before turning away to take the call.

THE DOORBELL RANG, ROUSING EARL FROM A DEEP SLEEP. He had just now fallen asleep. After a night filled with exciting memories, he had found it difficult to fall asleep immediately, the adrenaline making it hard for his body to calm down.

"Who is it?" He growled groggily, not pleased at being woken up this early. He planned on sleeping through the day and going out at night again, and he felt like a mess.

"So much work to be done and so little time."
Then he remembered that Bertha had promised to bring him some soup. He was glad he already looked like someone who was ill, what with his inability to fall asleep in time. It would not be hard for Bertha to believe that he was actually sick. He opened the door and stood in front of it, blocking anyone from seeing inside.

"Good morning, Earl." Bertha greeted loudly; her voice filled with cheer. He wondered how she could be so chipper very early in the morning and every day. He had yet to see Bertha having a bad day.

"Good morning, Bertha." He said, his voice raspy and low.

"I brought you soup like I promised I would. How do you feel this morning?" She asked, trying to look past his shoulder into the room. He straightened, blocking her view of the room.

"I feel much better, Bertha. Thank you for the soup." He said, reaching his hand for the bowl of soup. She handed it to him reluctantly, and Earl could tell that she was not pleased that he had not let her in.

"I am sorry, Bertha, I can't invite you in. My apartment is a mess, and I am ashamed for you to see it that way. I promise I will invite you once I feel better." He said, adding a note of shyness to his voice. This explanation seemed to be enough for Bertha because she immediately looked pacified.

"Alright, Earl. If you need anything, just let me know. Take care of yourself." She said, turning in her heels and heading out.

"Thank you, Bertha. I appreciate your kindness. Regards to your husband and kids." He called after her and then shut the door behind her. He set the Tupperware Bertha had given him on the counter beside the door. His apartment was clean. Earl was not willing to risk her stumbling upon anything incriminating he had not realized to clean up the previous night. He could never stand it being dirty; everything had to be in its place. He headed directly to the television, where the real reason he would not let anyone into his house was. His living room had an alcove in it. It was a space in the wall with an arched entrance. Earl had set a table up in that alcove where he had kept every empty cup of coffee Ciara had handed to him.

Whenever he ordered his coffee, she had a habit of signing his name on the cup with a red pen. She spelled his name, writing the letter 'R' with a thrill which ended in a heart shape at its tail. That was why he knew she was into him too. There was a large board on which he had pinned various pictures of Ciara. Ciara at work. Ciara at home. Ciara was walking home. Ciara was watering her plants. Working at the BMV had some perks. He had printed seven of Ciara's driver's license just for her picture and pinned them on his board too. He arranged them in such a way that they formed the number seven. On another board in the same alcove were pictures of those he had killed. He had found an old picture of Wrath and placed it at the top of the board. Sophia

Myer's picture was next; He placed a picture of hers from the yearbook beside one of the pictures he had taken of her dead body.

Next on the board was Julia Alvarez. Her driver's license registration picture and one picture of her dead body. He enjoyed this part of his life. Getting to look at the pictures and relive their deaths. Sometimes, he had to close his eyes to experience the feeling again but most times, just looking at the board was enough. He lay on the floor, looking up at his board of trophies.

He felt like a warrior who had captured trophies of war. Earl had read somewhere about the Native Americans who gave their young warriors titles based on the number of trophies they brought back from war. He could imagine himself in war paint only that his own war paint would be the blood of his trophies. The thought so excited him that he burst into laughter. He turned on the television. Earl watched the news, enjoying the confusion and fear the news anchors were portraying. He had not even known who her father was. 'Oh well…'

If they say it was a political statement, then it was. He alone knew he was fulfilling his destiny as the Chosen. It was even better if it put fear in other corrupt human beings' hearts. He chuckled and even burst out laughing at various points during the news where they made assumptions and guessed his actions' motives. He especially liked the pictures they were showing. Of course, they could not air the real pictures, but Earl had been there and knew exactly how everything looked.

"Call the detective," Duke demanded but Earl was hesitant.

That would definitely make things more interesting, but he disagreed with Duke; it would be too dangerous. He had slipped up when he called the last time; if it were not a burner phone he had managed off the internet months ago, then maybe they could have found him.

He went into his bedroom and opened his closet. His clothes were properly arranged by color and in sevens. He liked to have order in his life. At the back of the closet, Earl had installed a safe. He typed in his passcode and the safe clicked open. He had stashed a large amount of cash over the years. Lucky he had another phone there, two even. He took one of them, popped a sim card, and powered it on. He had written down the detective's personal cell number from the last time and quickly dialed the number. The detective picked up the call on the third ring which annoyed Earl a little. She should have been expecting his call and immediately pick up the call. He managed to compose himself and cheerfully said,

"Hello, Detective." The line was silent for a few seconds and Earl could picture her scrambling for a notepad or something like that. He chuckled. "I see you were not expecting me to call you."

The line still remained silent. If she was at the other end, he could not hear her, and Earl's composure was beginning to slip. She did not care for whatever he said if she was not answering him. He felt troubled.

"Well, I am sure you have received my note," Earl said, his voice becoming high pitched, and he cleared it in an effort to regain control.

"You don't get out much, do you?" The detective finally asked, her tone condescending. For as long as he had known, Earl had always hated being condescended to. He felt his head grow hot and squeezed the phone he held tight to his ear. "So… you're going to bullshit me again or what?"

"Don't talk to me like that-"

"I'll talk to you how I want to," She snapped, "you're messed up in the head and I'm not going to bullshit you with all the usual we want to help you crap. You've had your fun, so know this… I'll find you. And I'll fill you with lead before the judges get a chance to rule you insane. Thanks for calling, though- Now fuck off!" She replied and hung up on him.

Earl was shocked but then the rage burst out of him as he flung the phone at the wall and slammed his fist repeatedly into the wall after it. He wished he could see her, but the thought of how confident she might have been threatening him made him sick. He was the one in control; she had no right to speak to him that way.

One… Two… Three… Four… Five… Six… Seven…

He counted as he began to pace the room.

"I will show them what I am capable of."

…One… Two… Three… Four… Five…

I will unleash wrath and fear on these heathens carrying evil around.

…Six… Seven…

One…

CHAPTER
NINE

Anita stared at her cell phone when the call was disconnected. If her plan worked, then the next target would be herself, but that was only wishful thinking. In fact, she wondered why she had snapped like that. Dealing with sickos like the one she had just spoken to was exasperating. Pete walked into the office just then, a small folder in his hands.

"I was unable to reach the victim's father. According to his secretary, he is out of town on business." He stopped speaking, noticing her lack of response.

"The killer just called me." She said in a quiet voice.

"What?!" The nerve! Pete thought.

"Yes. And I think I pissed him off." Anita said, still staring off into the distance like it were nothing.

"What do you mean you pissed him off?" He asked, for the first time not caring that she was his superior.

"That is exactly what I meant." She replied, finally rousing herself. "He wanted to play games and I was not in the mood for any of it. I'm not exactly the most patient person, so I gave him a piece of my mind. He sounded pissed."

"Jesus, Detective what did you really say?"

"Nothing really… just said I was going to be the one to off him," She added as Pete stared puzzled at her. He could not tell if she was joking or if she really did threaten the killer. "Anything else from the Medical Examiner and Crime Scene unit?" she asked, seeming to have fully regained her composure. Pete was still reeling from the information she had given him. The guy was already unpredictable. He wondered what he would do now that he was angry.

"Nothing different from what they found the last time. The only thing was he tried to suffocate her with a pillow or something similar. Her airways were filled with fiber from a soft cloth material. He must have come prepared for one to fail as he promptly poured acid down her throat. As before, he had disfigured her face first while she was still alive." Pete read the file he had received from the medical examiner.

"And as before, this was not the murder site; it was only a dump site. They have not found the murder site yet." He finished, and Anita had not been expecting anything different.

"Anything about her clothing?" She asked, and Pete shook his head. They had not found her clothing anywhere yet.

"As of now, this has become a serial murder case. Unfortunately, we can only expect a break if he commits another murder. Seeing that he is angry, that would be sooner rather than later. Hopefully, he would slip up this time." Anita explained. It was sad, but Pete knew that they had hit a wall with all the information they had now.

IT WAS THE WEEKEND, WHICH WAS MEANT TO BE FREE TIME for her, but she had still gone to the precinct, leaving her kid with a neighbor. Justice could not afford to go on breaks. Until this case was solved and the killer caught, she could not allow herself to have a day off. She finally got the chance to look at the file Pete had sent her. She first saw the gruesome image of the woman's face. The face was disfigured as the number seven was carved crudely and not just on her forehead. It looked like the work of an unstable and angry person. Anita shook her head at the carnage. She quickly looked through the file and read that the woman had been a stranger in Crest Hill. A young boy who was mentally challenged found her and could not be of any use to the investigators. The legend of the dead woman in the woods was actually true, she thought.

Anita looked at the pictures, comparing the M.O. with that of the serial killer. It looked like a sloppy kill and must have been his first. She could easily match this murder with the two he had committed recently. One of the pictures caught her attention. She looked closely at the picture and gasped. A large dark mark, shaped like an apple, was on the woman's shoulder. She would know that birthmark anywhere.

Her mother had gone to the same spot as the dead woman.

She sat back in her chair; her hands were shaking and she was breathing hard. She had not heard from her mother since she had run away from home almost sixteen years ago. She did not know if she was alive or dead. She looked through the document one more time. The description of the boy sounded just like her little brother. She still regretted running away and leaving him behind, even after all these years. Now to see that he had possibly been on his own. If this woman really was her mother, Earl would have grown up alone with their scumbag of a father unless he left their mother or died. She hoped it was the latter.

The guilt gripped her heart, and she almost broke down in tears. She was glad Pete had left the office and she was alone. For now, she could not tell anyone that she was related to the first victim, and they would only take the case away from her. She had to find this killer. And then she would find her brother.

EARL WENT TO THE DINER FOR BREAKFAST. HE SAT AT HIS usual table and waited for Ciara to come out. He was sorely disappointed when her loud-mouthed friend Tonya came out instead. Earl was disappointed but hid his disdain with a smile.

"Hey, Earl!" She greeted in her loud voice. She did not seem to notice or care.

'Look at her. She nauseates me.'

"How have you been? Ciara's not in today. She went on a hot date with her boyfriend, Vinny." She leaned closer to him and whispered, grinning from ear to ear. She was the kind that gave way too much information out at once but for once, he was glad she did. "I think he is going to propose." She finished and squealed in delight as she poured him some coffee.

"What do you mean by she is on a date with Vinny? Who is this Vinny person?" He asked; Earl looked excited but deep down, he felt betrayed. It was like his world crumbling down- Again. Tonya looked puzzled.

"Vinny is only like her one true love. He's been her boyfriend for like two years. If you ask me, the proposal is long overdue." Tonya informed him.

'No one asked your opinion.'

Earl was speechless. He felt his heart pounding faster than normal, and his chest felt tight like someone had fit him into a vice and was crushing him. A myriad of thoughts ran through his head. He had not noticed Tonya was looking at him funny.

"Earl, are you alright?" She asked, her voice laced with concern.

'It is all your fault, you whore, ugly bitch. Yes. You are the reason she would run into another man's arms. How dare you stand here

and look at us like she cares when it is her who has caused this.'

He had overheard a conversation between Tonya and Ciara, and he was very sure she had influenced Ciara. "Yeah… Yeah, I'm great" He chuckled and ordered randomly off the menu. Earl was furious but somehow, he had managed to remain composed. It was almost as though he had become someone else.

That night, he could not sleep. He could not concentrate on anything. He kept seeing Ciara with another man. Now that he thought about it, he had met Vinny, and he saw him outside her house once. Earl had seen that Vinny guy at the diner a lot too. He should have known that something was wrong.

'It is just like high school all over. Like your sister leaving and your mother too.'

But he could not take Tonya's word for it. He knew she never liked him and had always tried to turn Ciara against him. He would wait for Ciara, and he would ask her himself. He stood up from his bed, restless and walked to his living room where the alcove was. He stared at pictures of Ciara, memorizing her facial features. Then the image of Vinny would materialize beside her, and he would become agitated again.

One thing was sure, and he knew exactly who was next already. He reached into his pocket and drew out his camera. Earl went into a dark room he had prepared just for this purpose. He had learned everything about photography and printing pictures on the internet. He brought out the memory card from his camera and proceeded to print the picture. When it was properly cured and dried, he took it back to his alcove and pinned it to the board.

'Bring an end to gluttony. The time had finally come.'

EARL FELL INTO A FITFUL SLEEP THAT NIGHT BUT COULD not sleep well. He had disturbing dreams. He was on the ranch again, a naive little boy clutching a bloodied shotgun while the Johnsons grimaced and hissed at him. '…They said, " we can't keep that monster here, " and he cried. "I didn't have a choice… he was hurting my mother," He pleaded and then a woman lumbered inhumanely towards him, her skin was bloated, and her forehead had the number 7 carved onto it. It was the first woman he killed; it was his mother and behind her was the legion of animals he had laid to waste in her place. 'You hurt me… you hurt me Earl', she muttered as he ran as fast as his legs could carry him. And yet no matter how fast he ran, he felt as though he were frozen in place with her rotting mouth breathing down his neck. He cried and shut his eyes just as the door before him was shut and they were all out. None of it made any sense; he knew nothing but fear and guilt and then-

'Earl…' a familiar voice gurgled as he spun to meet Sarah lying in a pool of vomit and blood, choking as foam bubbled up and out of her mouth; he rushed to her side crying and desperate to save her, holding her hand as she gave up and laid limply there. She was dead and it was all his fault. **'They are dead, and it is**

all your fault' Duke's voice turned again and again as Sarah's lifeless body gripped at his throat with foam spewing from her mouth, then another pair of hands gripped him from behind and another and another and another- And they were all marked there.

Earl sat up in his bed, breathing hard as though his heart threatened to burst within his chest. This dream again? He had not dreamt this dream in years. Why now?

He got out of bed and walked to his kitchen sink, where he drank a full glass of water. He checked the time and saw that it was barely 11 PM. He threw on a jacket over his flannel night clothes and left the apartment. He needed some air.

"I won't make that mistake again. I won't let anyone with the mark go Scot free." He whispered, hoping the breeze would take his thoughts to Sarah in the afterlife. He had failed once by letting a marked sinner go free, and not this time. He stepped out into the night and aimlessly strolled about town for a while before returning to his apartment and falling asleep much easier.

"Tomorrow is another day. Tomorrow I will add a trophy to my collection." were his thoughts as he pulled himself to sleep.

It had been two weeks had gone by and there had been two murders, yet no clues had surfaced to lead them in the right direction.

"This has to end soon. We cannot have a raving lunatic walking around Scot free. Imagine the embarrassment? He is even in contact with you." Chief Doyle shouted, his voice bouncing around his small office.

Anita had just reported the last call she had with the person she supposed was the killer to the Police Chief and he had been surprised. The mayor was breathing down his neck to get this thing solved. People were beginning to panic and call the police station incessantly. Doyle was afraid that if this continued, he would have a serial killer on his hands and a rioting town too.

"We are doing all we can, sir. We have found a cold case that is similar to his murders now. A Jane Doe was found dead close to the High school more than ten years ago, and the MO and the markings on the victim's face are similar." Anita said. She avoided his eyes, feeling ashamed that all this could be happening under her watch.

Anita had not told anyone about her suspicions about the identity of the first victim.

Nothing on the bodies had given a tangible clue as to how they could find the killer. They had not found the second murder scene yet and the only thing they had were the notes the killer had sent with the dead people. And the calls.

He had taken to calling her at least once each day to taunt her.

"You can never find me, even when I am right under your nose. I have a mission to fulfill, and the forces protect me." He had boasted just the day before. Anita had gritted her teeth to stop herself from insulting him or calling him names. She kept hoping that he would slip up and give her a clue as to who he was or where he was.

All she had heard was that he was on a mission, a self-righteous mission to purge the world of evil.

What kind of demented mind thought what he was doing was making the world a better place? Anita thought. The past week had been a real struggle for her, and she had to keep reminding herself of the reason why she had become sober, or she would be forced to go back to drinking.

Her daughter was her motivation not to go back to drinking. This case and the sick bastard were testing her resolve. Anita had come to expect his call almost every night.

Just then, a call came in for the chief who looked up at her.

"Get this thing solved and bring it to an end, Ann." He instructed then took a deep breath before picking up the phone.

"Hello, Mr. Mayor…" Anita left, not wanting to hear the rest of the conversation.

EARL SAT AT HIS DESK TRYING TO WORK BUT NOT succeeding. An incessant buzz in his brain kept distracting him from doing anything. He rubbed his temple trying to stop the buzz, but it persisted.

He fidgeted in his seat, trying to get comfortable but that did not help either. Sweat began to pour down his face onto his tabletop and the papers he was trying to work on. He looked at the time and sighed. It was almost closing time, and he could go home and help himself to some boosters. At five minutes to closing time, Kyle came out of his own office and stepped into Earl's office. As usual, he walked like he owned the place which Earl found really annoying.

"Employee of the month. It seems you have begun to lag in your work. I can see you have not dotted an 'I' here and you have missed out the applicant's date of birth." He said, pointing at the paper he was working on. The disdain Earl heard in his voice made him pause. He gritted his teeth but did not look up.

"Why, thank you Kyle for noticing." He said sweetly through gritted teeth. He made the corrections and filed the papers.

"I wonder how you have been able to win Employee of the Month for three months consecutively. Are you giving Jim gifts? Or do you have a way of lobbying that I do not know about? Because I know you are not capable of doing this yourself." Kyle said, sitting at the edge of Earl's chair and holding his chin as if he was in deep thought.

"You have always been a bumbling idiot." Kyle continued then laughed loudly at his lame joke.

"Stop that, Kyle. Why are you being so cruel? You are acting like a child, not an adult." Bertha said, coming to Earl's defense.

'*This guy has got to go.*' Duke grumbled but Earl did not humor him; as annoying as Kyle was, he did not have the mark. He did not deserve to die. As Earl was packing up to leave the office, he looked up at Kyle who was still laughing. Then as he hoped, the mark had appeared on his forehead. And for the first time, Earl genuinely smiled at Kyle. A chill went through Kyle's body at Earl's cold smile and he immediately stopped laughing. He could not tell why but felt uncomfortable being there, so he quietly left Earl's office. He had gotten enough laughs for one day. Earl's mood was suddenly improved.

"Bye, Bertha. See you tomorrow." He said, waving at her as he walked out of the office. He walked to the parking lot just as Kyle was reaching for his car keys. He opened his car and hopped in. The car was one of the things Kyle bragged about. It was the Honda Ridgeline. It was Earl's dream car, but he could not afford it yet. Earl knew Kyle could not afford the car. Not on his salary. It must be good to have a trust fund. It was the latest model. Granted, the truck was a powerful vehicle with a V6 3.5-liter engine, six cylinders, and a 280 at six thousand horsepower among other features. It made Earl's small Toyota look like a grocery store cart.

Kyle started his engine and put his car in gear at the same time Earl was backing out of his parking space. The cars would have nearly collided if it were not for Earl's quick and better judgment. He stopped his car before the collision could happen. Kyle honked and stuck his head out through his window.

"Look where you are going you son of a bitch!" He shouted and flipped Earl off, then sped off.

Oh, enjoy this while you can. I am coming for you.

HE WENT DIRECTLY TO THE CREST HILL DINER. Thankfully, Ciara was there. He was not sure he could keep his mood up if he had met Tonya alone. He was also going to confirm from her if Tonya had been telling the truth, and it would mean she had been lying to him and stringing him along all this while, just like Sophia had in high school.

"Hey, Earl!" Ciara greeted when she saw him. He was excited, and she would not greet him with such affection and fondness if she had been cheating on him.

"Hey, Ciara. You didn't tell me you wouldn't be in yesterday." He said, trying to keep the accusation out of his tone.

"Oh. Yeah. I had something very important to attend to. I hope Tonya treated you well?" She said with a large grin on her face.

The diner door opened, and Vinny came into Earl's dismay. Immediately he did, Ciara turned away from Earl and went to him. She put her hands around his neck and Earl winced as she kissed him. It felt like he had a knife thrust into the back of his neck. Painfully disgusting. Vinny held her close to him.

She had not even waited to hear his answer. It was true. She had been lying to him all this while. All her affectionate pet names had been fake, and they had all been lies- Ciara did not love him. Earl felt his heart drop and could barely let out a breath for a few minutes. He became lightheaded and had to lay his head on the counter.

"Earl. Are you alright?" He heard Ciara ask in concern.

'Don't ask us that; you are lying, cheating slut.'

"Yeah, I am. Just a little lightheaded, I guess," Was what he actually said, raising his head from the countertop. "Who's that?" He asked her after he had calmed down a bit.

"Come on Earl. You know Vinny. My boyfriend, well, fiancé now. He proposed yesterday," Ciara said with so much excitement as she flashed a ring in his face. She squealed and he smiled. Earl tried not to show the disdain he actually felt. He let out mirthless laughter and looked down at her hand. The ring was lovely with a large diamond on it.

"Wow!" was all he could manage to say. "This is huge. Congratulations, Ciara." He choked out and abruptly got up from his seat, ready to leave.

"Come on, let me introduce you guys," Ciara said, gesturing for Vinny to come closer.

"Hey, love, I want you to meet Earl, my regular customer. Earl, this is Vinny, my fiancé." She said. Vinny held his hand for a handshake, and Earl took it and shook it briefly.

"Nice to meet you, Vinny. Congratulations." He said and quickly left.

'Regular customer? How dare she?'

Earl wanted to say something but could only muster a greeting as he excused himself. He wanted to be as far away from them as possible- Ciara had the mark too.

His mind was in a whirl and his emotions were all over the place. He went home to his apartment and went directly to the alcove where he had built a shrine for her. He stood in front of the table looking over the pictures and the cups on which she had inscribed his name lovingly. He hesitated. He traced his fingers over them as tears pooled under his eyelids; not again! He roared as he raised his fist and swept them all to the ground but then he held himself. He was furious but could not bring himself to destroy the shrine. It was not her fault. Ciara would never seek to hurt him; he had failed her, he had failed another person and now she was marked. But it was not their fault; Vinny was to blame.

Vinny was the culprit here. Vinny and Tonya. They must have filled Ciara's head with garbage. They must have contaminated her and made her just like them. He had never seen the mark on her before. He remembered how his mother had been helpless against his father's cruelty and had ultimately been infected by the evil he carried because Earl had not killed his father in time. Yes, he had saved his mother from Tom Hughes but not ultimately from the evil that Tom had carried. Now the same was happening with his Ciara. He had to put an end to this, and he had to save her. Ciara was pure. She had a pure heart and had been chosen to be his. He had to rid her of Vinny and Tonya before she worsened.

Earl was sure Ciara could be redeemed if they were no longer around her. He had to do this and act fast. He resolved to help Ciara once he had dealt with envy. It was time to work. He dressed in a black hoodie and stashed his chisel in his pocket. His little get-up had become sort of like a uniform to him. The uniform of the chosen. He was about to leave the house but on second thought, decided that he was going to need more than a blow to the head to deal with this particular menace. He opened his safe and brought out a small .38 mm gun he had bought a few years back. Now that he thought about it, he got this gun with the intention of blowing his own brains out; the universe had subtly been preparing him for this day.

He would use it only if necessary. He liked working with his hands than with weapons. That was why he found it hard to count Tom among his trophies. It had not been done with finesse, and he had still been a young boy who had barely understood the assignment he had been given. Now, he was getting better and better at planning and executing. This time, he had something planned that would be sensational. He was sure his trophy would appreciate it as much as the police would.

Earl chuckled as he let himself out of his house.

He would not need to drive today. He would just walk. Earl had checked this guy's address before leaving the office and was not far from his house. Kyle lived in a two-bedroom house on Crescent Street alone. This made things a lot easier. He approached the house from the main entrance, walking up the driveway as if he belonged there. The porch light was on so anyone who was passing by could see him or any nosy neighbor could see him. But Earl had covered up nicely. No one would be able to identify him even if they saw him.

He could hear loud music coming from inside the house and wondered what the celebration was for, especially since Kyle was alone. He was willing to bet that Kyle's neighbors hated him as much as he did. Who plays music so loud at this time of the night, if not a self-absorbed fool who thinks the world owes him everything?

Whichever way anyone liked to look at things, Earl was doing everybody a favor. It may not be through conventional means, but this was the permanent way. Earl went to the door and jiggled the lock. He was not bothered that anyone would hear him. It did not budge. He brought out two thin wires and picked the lock, easily opening the door in seconds. He walked into the house. He stood just inside the door and watched Kyle dance wildly in nothing but his underwear. Kyle's dance would have made Earl laugh in a different situation but not this. Here he only felt like hacking his head off and leaving. He watched for almost five minutes before Kyle sensed someone was in the house with him. When he noticed, he shouted and almost tripped on his white, expensive-looking couch. He had bottles of beer lying around and one in his hand.

"Who…who are you and what are you doing in my house. How did you get in here?" He asked, his eyes going from Earl to the door and back.

"Don't tell me you do not recognize me, Kyle?" Earl said, slowly approaching Kyle who had regained his stamina and was now standing. He looked like a deer caught in headlights, which made Earl quite excited. Kyle could not understand that the almost demonic voice was coming from a familiar face. Earl could almost smell the fear coming off of Kyle. The guy was a loudmouth and a bully, so it was funny to see him cowering in fear in his own home.

"The fuck Earl! What are you doing here?" Kyle stammered, stepping backward towards his stairs. Earl kept approaching him until his legs encountered the sofa and he plopped into it.

"Where is all your bravado now, Kyle?" Earl asked, moving his face menacingly closer to Kyle's.

"I do not… not… kn… know what you are talking about?" Kyle asked again

"You will know soon enough. Now get dressed!" Earl commanded.

"Where are you taking me to? I am not going anywhere with you." Kyle said, trying to resist. Earl quietly pulled out the gun he had out in his pocket and pointed it at Kyle. He screamed like a lit

"Get the fuck up and get dressed or I will blow your fucking brains all over this beautiful couch," Earl said again, this time with less force. He did not want to get into a scuffle with him here, and that was going to leave too much evidence. Kyle scrambled off the couch and went into his bedroom, Earl following him with the gun. Kyle wore the clothes he had worn to work that day and his shoes.

Earl gestured with the gun for him to walk out of the room and to the living room, then stood right behind him.

"Now where are your truck keys?" Earl asked.

"If that is all you want, you can have it. I don't need it anymore. Just don't hurt me." Kyle started crying and handed the keys to Earl.

"You disgust me," Earl said, looking at the man who tormented him in high school and continued with his torment even as an adult. Here he was crying like a baby.

"Now we are going to walk out of here like buddies. I will not hesitate to cap you if you make any wrong move." He said, holding Kyle around the shoulders and holding the gun to his side, under his jacket. They both walked out of the house. Earl instructed him to lock the door, which he did. He walked Kyle to the car, which was parked at the side of the house where there was no light.

Kyle opened the car and Earl shoved him into the backseat and tied his hands and legs. Then knocked him in the head with his fist, knocking Kyle unconscious.

Earl took the driver's seat and began driving, whistling as he drove.

'Woah, this car is a dream to drive. Too bad it belonged to the bastard who was destined to die.'

Earl parked the truck at the intersection leading out of town. He was far enough from the main town not to be heard and close enough to walk back without being detected. He came down from the truck and looked behind, and Kyle was still unconscious. He dragged the guy out of the car and took him to a large tree. Earl had parked the car where no one would see them, but close enough to the road for the body to be noticed early. He stripped Kyle of his clothes and tied him to the tree. He then proceeded to chisel the number 7 on his forehead. Kyle woke up then, screaming in pain. When Earl had finished, Kyle was sobbing so hard, and he had shit himself.

"This is disgusting." He said, scrunching his nose from the smell.

"Please, what have I done to you? I will pay you all the money you want. Just let me go. You can have the car, and I don't care. Just please have mercy on me. Let me go." He begged.

"It is too late for you, Kyle. You cannot receive any mercy at this point. You bullied and insulted people right from when you were a kid. You did not outgrow your need to put others down to feel good about yourself. You still made me feel inferior to you, even knowing that you handed your work over to your subordinates while you did nothing. You do not deserve this job; you were given the job because you have connections. Yet, you are a lazy, good-for-nothing, envious son of a bitch. It ends here and now."

Kyle tried to open his eyes wider against the glare of the truck's headlights.

"Earl. Earl, please… aren't we buddies?" He asked, and Earl did not answer him. Earl drew Kyle up on his feet.

"Earl, please don't do this. I know I'm a dirtbag, but I don't deserve this. No one deserves this, Earl. Please let me go." Kyle begged but Earl was not listening.

He had tied his back to the tree in a kneeling position but drew him up to his full height and secured the knot behind him to the tree.

Earl then returned to the truck, got in and revved the engine. Realizing Earl's intent, Kyle's eyes widened, and he struggled against the rope.

"Please…don't do this, Earl." He begged, the tears pouring in rivulets down his cheeks. The last thing Kyle saw, was Earl's eyes. It was filled with pure evil. Earl revved the engine again and accelerated. Kyle's body slumped forward when the truck made an impact on him. Earl jerked forward and laughed, he had forgotten to put on the seatbelt, and once he did, he reversed and accelerated again, hitting Kyles, doubled over the body. He slammed into the body five more times and only stopped cause the car had been coated in too much gore and had been deformed by the tree. Then he came out of the car, leaving what was left of the headlights on to illuminate the bloodied pulp that was left of him between the car and the tree it was strung to.

Kyle's last spotlight.

CHAPTER
TEN

Anita walked into the third crime scene in seventeen days. Pete was right beside her. The first thing she noticed was that this time, the gimmick was different. "He's either done playing games or this wasn't a plan." She said to Pete, who nodded, looking around. The killer had picked a spot just outside of town but within walking distance from the main town.

"To think that this killer lives among us."

Crest Hill was a small town with a population of barely four thousand people. It was a scary notion that someone among them could be doing this and enjoying it. They seldom had new people move into town either, so this person may be someone they all knew in one way or the other. They may have bumped into each other at the bank or even the precinct. The thought caused a shudder to run through Pete.

"The victim is Kyle Sanders, a Twenty Eight-year-old native who works at the BMV. This is his car." A crime scene tech approached them and explained to them.

"Woah… do they earn enough to afford this kind of truck?" Anita asked with a chuckle but did not get an answer. They all considered it uncalled for, but she did not care. She would look into it later. "Anything on him to show us who did this?"

"Nothing yet. Besides, we would have to take him to the medical examiner's office to be able to determine the real cause of death." The woman told her.

"Let us look around the car," Anita said to Pete while pulling on her gloves. She checked the back seat and found nothing interesting. They would need to dust the car for print, but she was almost sure he would not have left any prints.

"Over here!" Pete called, having crouched at the other side of the car. Anita approached him and saw what he was looking at. There was a piece of black fiber caught between the car door and the handle. Anita's heart began to pound. For once, it looked like they had evidence. She tried not to get too excited because this may very well belong to the victim. From what she could see of him, he was naked, so she could not determine if the fiber came from his clothes or the killer's clothes.

She called for a crime scene tech to bag the evidence and then opened the driver's side door. She first saw a small sheet of paper on the seat, and she picked it up and read what he had written on it.

HERE LAY THE FOURTH- KYLE SANDERS-POSTER KID FOR ENVY

HE DESERVED TO DIE. HE SHOULD NEVER HAVE BEEN BORN.

Anita sighed again, showing Pete the piece of paper. He took it and read what had been written, and he hissed in frustration and then raised the paper closer to his face.

"I think I can see something inscribed in this paper," Pete said. Anita rushed to his side.

"What do you see?" She asked frantically.

"I am not sure, but we may need a magnifying glass, and I have one in my drawer at the precinct," Pete said and headed to his squad car. Anita got in with him and they drove off to the precinct. Her cell phone rang while they were still in the car.

"Hello." She said, trying her best not to pour out her frustrations. She wanted to keep him talking as long as possible, and she wanted him to slip up about something. The moment he noticed an attitude in her voice, he usually hung up the phone.

"Hi, Detective Heath, my good friend. I keep dropping you presents but you never return the favor." He said, actually giggling. This guy was really sick.

"That's because I don't have your address." She said with a calm voice.

"You don't have to know my address. You can keep my present anywhere and make sure the news captures it. I will pick it up then." He spoke. Was he seriously thinking she owed him a gift?

"But you are leaving dead people around. These people have families, you know." She said.

"I have told you before that they deserve to die supersedes anything else. Every other consideration is an unnecessary one." He replied.

"You are just a sick, demented bastard with a god complex too big for you. We will get you and so, help me, God, and I will kill you with my own bare hands." Anita said. The line went dead before she had finished speaking.

Shit!

"You need to be the calm detective. Don't let him get under your skin. That is exactly the reaction he wants from you." Pete said, trying to calm her. "We are going to get him. He is getting much more confident and that in itself is a slip-up."

Anita knew what he meant but that did not make it an easier pill to swallow.

At the precinct, Pete looked at the paper again under his magnifying glass. The paper had been engraved with the BMV logo, and that could mean he had used the victim's writing materials since they knew he worked at the BMV.

Looking a little further to the right, Pete noticed a smudged fingerprint.

"I can see a fingerprint, but it is smudged." He informed Anita who came closer to see what he was talking about.

"Send this to the crime scene unit immediately. Let them know it is urgent. In fact, stay with them until they give you a result." She told him, and Pete quickly bagged it and proceeded to do as she had asked.

This bastard was going down sooner rather than later.

EARL WALKED INTO THE OFFICE VERY CHEERFUL. Everything was proceeding as planned. The only thing that wanted to spoil his mood was the detective's response. She had not been friendly; all he had done was keep her informed. They were both fighting the same battle only because he had divine backing while she was just using her limited faculties. He had only wanted to make things easier for her. Without him, she would not have found these people who were worse criminals than junkies or burglars. These were criminals for whom no penalties exist in the human laws.

He sighed and mentally shrugged his shoulders. He had known many would not understand him, but he had hoped the detective would.

He sat at his desk before looking around. Bertha was not in yet, which was rather strange. She was usually the first to come into the office every day. He shrugged again and proceeded with his activities for the day. He knew they had already heard about Kyle, but he was going to pretend he did not.

About thirty minutes later, Bertha walked into the office, her eyes and nose red.

"Hello Bertha. How are you doing?" He asked her, and she nodded but did not answer him. "Bertha, are you fine? What is wrong with you?" He asked, standing up to approach her desk.

"You haven't heard?" She asked him. He looked at her looking like he was clueless.

"Kyle was murdered during the night. That murderer who had killed two women earlier got to him too." She said and burst into tears.

"My goodness! What a pity." He said, rubbing Bertha's back and trying to comfort her.

"Oh, Kyle. What did Kyle ever do to anyone to deserve this kind of death?" She asked while sobbing. It was all he could do not to smack her in the head.

'Kyle was a brute, and you know it. He was the worst bully with a large helping of entitlement. And he deserved to die like he did, over and over again.'

But he continued to try and console her. It was laughable that they all thought the world of him now that he was dead but hated his guts while he had been alive—fickle human beings. Jim came into the office, and they did a kind of memorial for Kyle.

A colleague, friend, and man of integrity.

AFTER WORK, HE WENT TO EAT AT CREST HILL DINER AS usual. He had not seen hide nor hair of Vinny in a while and had begun to relax. Ciara still wore his ring, but Earl felt it in his guts that Vinny was trying to deceive her and did not really love Ciara. All he wanted to do was breed the spawn of the devil in Ciara.

Earl was not going to let that happen. But for now, he had to lay low. He had heard on the news that the police had found some evidence. He did not know what it was and was sure he covered his tracks well, but he could not be so sure. He was going to take his time and just live, be near Ciara as much as he could. Very likely, he could neutralize Vinny's influence on her and redeem her by being near her. Then he would permanently deal with both Vinny and Tonya.

"Hi, Earl," Ciara said as he walked into the diner. She smiled brightly at him, making his heart leap in his chest. He could imagine her beautiful lips joining with his and her arms wrapped around his waist.

'Oh, Bliss.'

She was so beautiful that Earl felt his breath leave his lungs. It was almost like he saw her for the first time every day. But she still had the mark on her.

"Hello, Ciara." He said, having to clear his throat so he would not give away his thought. He averted his eyes so she would not see how dilated they were both from cocaine and his lustful thoughts about her.

"Will you have your usual?" She asked him and he nodded. She poured him a cup of coffee and went to prepare his food. He watched her walk away liking the way her hips moved. He felt a tightening in his pants and had to take deep breaths to calm himself. Just then, Vinny walked in, and all thoughts of Ciara's lips and hips flew out of his mind and were replaced with anger and murder. The guy swaggered into the diner like he owned the place. He walked to the counter, tapped on it, and then looked towards where he was sitting.

"Oh hi, Ear…l, right?" He said, walking towards where Earl was seated. He stretched out his hand for a shake and Earl shook him, albeit reluctantly. Vinny pulled up a seat and sat beside Earl, and Ciara brought his food just then.

"Oh hey, babe!" She exclaimed, looking at Vinny with so much affection.

"Hey, you too." He said and hugged her over the counter, kissing her smack on the lips. When his hand landed on her backside and rested there was when Earl saw red.

'How dare this pervert to touch her in public like that. In front of us.'

It was as if Vinny was rubbing insult on injury. He could not understand how long he had wished for an opportunity to hold her just like that and to have her arms wrapped around him. He turned his eyes away from them but could not eat anymore. He left immediately after that giving Ciara a lame excuse about why he had to go. He returned home and sat in front of his shrine to Ciara, but this time he could not focus on her face. He looked at the board with his victim's pictures. He had added Kyle before and after to the board. Tonya was next then Vinny. But he may have to change the order of things seeing that Vinny was becoming more and more of a problem that needed to be urgently taken care of.

He stared at the picture of the handsome man. He was undoubtedly a lovely specimen of humanity, but all Earl could see was slothfulness. Tonya had said he owned a business but how come he was always at the diner hovering around Ciara like flies to a rotting corpse?

Wrong analogy. Ciara could not be compared to something so distasteful.

"But you know what I mean, right?"

'Yes, I do. We need to handle it and quickly.' *Duke growled.*

He stood up from where he had been sitting in front of his memorial to Ciara and walked to the kitchen. He found his supply of cocaine and took a healthy snort; He was about to run out, and he needed to call his dealer. Tomorrow.

DETECTIVE ANITA STOOD BESIDE LOGAN MILLER AS THEY watched the computer algorithm sort through the system for the owner of the partial fingerprint, they had uncovered at the crime scene.

It had been especially hard to extract the print from the paper but after carefully examining the paper, they had managed it. Now, all that remained was for them to find out to whom it belonged.

"We have questioned everyone at the BMV except one guy who was not around today. His colleague said he had taken sick leave and did not come in that day." Pete said as he walked into Logan's office. He had been on the field all morning trying to question as many people as possible and for this particular victim, they had a lot of people to talk to. He must have been quite popular.

"From what most of the neighbors say, he was antisocial and quite rude. On the night of his murder, he had been playing loud music late into the night." He told Anita.

"Why hadn't anyone reported him?" She asked. Pete shrugged.

"They were most likely tired of reporting. I found several complaints in our files against Mr. Kyle Sanders. Apparently, he must have had a lot of people who hated his guts and caught the killer's attention." Pete explained.

"All his victims seem random so far. Something must connect them. At least the killer must have encountered them in one way or the other to know about their characters." Anita said.

"I am still looking through records to see if they all have a common person or incident. We are yet to find something that links them together, except that Sophia and Kyle went to the same High School. But I have a gut feeling that none of them are random targets to me." Pete told her.

"That link is what we need to find." She finished. "Why is this taking so long?" She asked Logan.

"The print we lifted is partial. The system has to take its time to search and find a complete one. Give it some more time." Logan said.

We don't have much time, Anita thought knowing there was nothing they could do but wait.

"Has he called you again?" Pete asked her.

"Nope. It had been silent from his side, and I think he is done talking. We can expect an onslaught of activities." She said, and Pete understood exactly what she meant by "activities."

"Make sure there are policemen on every street corner tonight." She instructed Pete. No sleep for any policeman until this perp is caught, preferably today.

EARL CROUCHED OUTSIDE THE DINER, WAITING FOR HER. He had decided that he would not go to work at least for the rest of the week, and he had to complete everything before anything went wrong.

Earlier, he had silently watched as she locked the door to the diner, oblivious to him. He did not mind that. At least for now, he had to remain in the shadows. The time would come for her to know him and his true intentions, his love for her. She already knew him, but she was yet to know how intertwined their lives are.

She was dressed in long pants and a thick jacket on a cold night. He had noticed she was wearing a plaid shirt underneath the jacket when he had been sitting at the counter and she had served him. And as usual, she had smiled at him when she had refilled his mug. If that was not an indication that she loved him, he did not know what was. She was the most beautiful woman he had ever met in his life. Her long black hair had blonde streaks in it, a touch he liked so much. Her eyes were large and brown, and he could see everything she was feeling. That was how he had known that she had fallen in love with him. Her eyes always lit up whenever he walked into the diner, and she always seemed to be making fresh coffee.

She was beautiful and petite and would fit perfectly into his arms. He liked that. He always followed her from work. Just to keep her safe, nothing else. He knew her route and was glad she was into routines just as he was. They were practically soul mates. He made his steps match with hers from the other side of the road where he was walking in the shadows. She had a spring in her steps every day and he was sure it was because she knew he was there to keep her safe. He was just like her guardian angel.

He knew her house was a few blocks away from her diner because he always paid attention to her. They had walked this same path together, every day, for almost three weeks now. It was a straight route, with no corners or turns, which he was very comfortable with. But today, she took a detour. At first, Earl could not believe it. She never took a detour. Their relationship hinged on the fact that they were both creatures of habit…routines.

'I told you. She's just like Sophia.' Duke's raspy voice sounded in his ears. He shook his head, trying to dispel it.

"No. She's different, and she really loves me, just as much as I love her." He whispered to Duke.

"Shut up! She isn't!" He whispered to Duke. Instead of shutting up, Duke broke out in uncontrollable laughter which annoyed him. He could barely contain the urge to hit himself on the head seven times and resorted to tapping on his thighs seven times. That was the only way to get rid of Duke. That and counting. By the time he was done, he felt better, and Duke's voice was gone but so was she.

He heaved a sigh of relief and walked on. She could not be anywhere else, and he knew exactly where she lived. After all, what kind of man would he be if he did not keep his woman safe.

He stood outside her apartment and waited. He just watched and did nothing else.

Just then, she returned to the apartment, but she was not alone. She had another man with her, a tall, muscular man holding her around the shoulders.

"Vinny." He whispered, his voice full of venom.

Duke's scornful laughter started again, and he was screaming, ***"I told you."*** over and over again.

He watched as Vinny and Ciara walked down the street towards her apartment. It grated on him that she was so comfortable with him, and he was touching her all over her body, which made him uncomfortable. No one but him should hold Ciara in such a way.

He watched them kiss and Ciara entered the house while Vinny watched.

"Like what you see?" Duke's voice smirked as Earl turned his back to the house and sulked. Duke would not shut up, nagging Earl as he walked away from her house. Earl's chest hurt so badly that he had to hold his hand over it to steady himself. His heart felt like it had burst, he was heartbroken. When Earl refused to answer Duke returned to taunting him, laughing viciously as Earl banged his hand against his head seven times to shut him up.

"No. He just walked her to her house, and she did not do anything wrong. That kiss can't mean anything." He whispered to himself. If anything, he needed to do better in taking care of his woman.

"She's sweet, and sweet things always attract ants. That's what he is… an ant, a pest!" Earl said.

"You saw it, didn't you?"

"For once, Duke you have a point; it makes perfect sense now. Vince… is evil. I saw it, the mark. He has the mark on his forehead." Earl said.

As soon as she was in, Vinny turned around and left. Earl had found out that he owned a gym on the other side of town, so he followed him.

Tonya should have been next, but she had gone out of town. Leaving Vinny. He had to take care of that now. The gym was fully equipped but thankfully, no one was in. It was almost midnight after all. Vinny had a studio apartment above his gym, where he lived. Earl looked around the building and found a small door that he could easily break into. He crept up the stairs to Vinny's apartment. So far, Vinny was not aware that anyone had followed him. He had not locked his door most likely thinking his gym was locked and no one would have access to his apartment. Earl slipped in through the open door and then hid behind a curtain. Vinny walked out of the bathroom, a towel wrapped around his waist, still dripping from his shower. The man looked strong, and Earl knew he had his work cut out for him. He would not be able to take him out.

Everything would have to take place here.

Earl crept out of his hiding place towards Vinny's bedroom, where he could hear him whistling as he dressed up. He crept up behind him and waited there with a baseball bat he had taken from beside the door; Vinny did not know what hit him till the bat came crashing down at the back of his head. If it were anyone else, their skull might have been split open like a coconut, but Vinny was strong; he could take a hit. He just was not expecting this one. Vinny fell face forward to the ground but struggled to regain his bearing and stay conscious. Earl panicked and swung again but Vinny caught the bat and sent him railing into the wall with a blow to his chin. Earl was dizzy and his head spun when Vinny swung his arms around him like a snake and put him in a chokehold quicker than he could relapse. Earl struggled but his vision waned; this was how it would end 'NEVER!!!'

A newfound strength flushed through Earl and like a man possessed, he took the chisel from his pocket and plunged it into Vinny's right eye. Vinny shoved him away roaring in pain as he clutched the chisel; it was lunge so deeply that he was too afraid to take it out. "My God!!!" He yelled as his other eye opened just as he saw Earl take the baseball bat, "Wait..it was you?" He gasped in shock as the bat came down on the chisel in his head, plunging it deeper into his skull, then again on the side of his chin, smashing his jaw, then again on his forehead and neck, and again and again and again until his body was unrecognizable. Earl paused when his arms began to feel sore.

Vinny became still. With the chisel's handle bulging out of his head, and he was dead.

Earl looked at his face in the mirror and saw that he was bleeding.

"Shit!" He exclaimed.

He had expended his anger on Vinny. Earl was pissed.

When he had calmed down, he pulled the chisel out of Vinny's skull and sat on the floor to survey what he had done.

'What have you done?'

There was nothing neat about this kill and though Duke was worried, all he did was laugh. **'You've screwed us. This wasn't right'**

He stared into the mirror and smirked. Duke must have been the scared one for once, and Earl took glee in that fact as he left the apartment. Strolling without a care in the world as though he were not covered in blood. He had forgotten to be careful.

Nothing else mattered.

Earl realized that Duke may have been his messenger. But he was the real deal, and **he was GOD.**

"WE HAVE FOUND A MATCH FOR YOUR FINGERPRINT," Logan said to Anita.

"You have? Do you have an identity?" She asked, afraid to hope.

"Yes. His name is Earl Hughes." Logan said, reading from his file. Anita's heart sank. Earl Hughes? Her brother was the one doing this? She turned aside so that no one would see her face.

"He was born in Crest Hill. His mother had killed his father and was put in jail, and he became a ward of the state then." Logan explained.

"I will email you the rest of his profile," Logan said. Anita managed to nod and then walked out of the M.E's office.

In minutes, Anita received Logan's email. There was another page with the killer's information.

The face she saw did not look like it belonged to a person who could carry out such heinous crimes. And it was her brother, alright. She read through his profile and saw a young man who had gone through a lot of hurts, especially from those who were supposed to protect him, coupled with bad choices. She read through the document and was almost moved to pity at what he had been through. His victim's faces materialized in her mind's eye and her heart became hardened. This was not the cute little boy she knew, who followed her all over the place and called her

"Ann." This was a monster, and he stopped being her brother long ago. Justice must be served.

She dialed Pete's phone.

"Get a squad, and we have our perp." She said as soon as he picked up. It was late at night but most of the cops were still in. Everyone was ready in a few minutes, their faces filled with a mix of anticipation and anger.

This had to end tonight.

EARL DECIDED AGAINST GOING TO HIS HOUSE, AND HE decided that he would go to Ciara. Now she would see how much he loved her and how far he was willing to go to save her. He knocked on her door and she opened it. She was surprised to see him. To the best of her knowledge, she had never invited Earl to her home. How did he know where she lived?

Besides that, he looked like someone who had been in a fight. His shirt was stained with blood and his eye was already swollen. "Earl! What are you doing here? What happened to you?" she asked him, moving back. He took it as an invitation to enter and stumbled in. He whirled round to face her. Ciara was scared. His eyes looked wild. She had never seen him look like this and wondered how he had come to know her house. Earl paused and hesitated. He had felt this way for a long time and now he finally had his chance.

"Ciara, I love you." He said earnestly, looking at her and willing her to understand. If she looked him in the eye, then she would understand. If she looked him deep in his bloody eye, then she would see how much love he had for her. She recoiled and stared disdainfully at him.

"Earl, what do you mean? You know I have a fiancé." She said, trying to reason with him. Ciara wanted to believe Earl's obvious infatuation for her had passed. She had a feeling this was not going to end well. "I'm sorry I can't-"

"But you can you see," Earl corrected gleefully. "Vinny's dead, so you're free."

"Oh my God… what did you say?" She gasped and paled as she backed away from Earl. Earl was confused, and she did not sound as excited as he thought she would and neither did she seem inviting; he almost had to force his way in with how tight the passage she left him was.

"I killed him for you, Ciara. He was only going to use you to conceive the devil's spawn." He spoke.

"What do you mean he's dead? You killed him?" She asked in unbelief as he smiled and nodded at her. She turned and ran to her table where she had kept her phone. Her body felt heavy, but she needed to move. No wonder he had not been replying to her messages. She tried to call him and then she heard his ringtone from behind her. It came from inside Earl's hoodie.

"Earl, what did you do, you sick bastard." He approached her, already pulling out his bloody chisel.

"Why'd you call him? Would I ever lie to you?" He asked but she ran to the other side of the room, already dialing 911.

"911, what's your emergency?" The operator said.

"Help, He has a …" She could not complete her statement when Earl slammed her head against the wall, knocking her unconscious.

"How could she do this to us? We did everything for her." He berated himself, "HOW COULD SHE!"

He looked at her unconscious form on the floor. Her beautiful face looked peaceful, except for the small gash he had hit her. He carried her limp body into the bedroom and laid her gently on the bed.

'We have to complete what we have started. She is no longer of use to us, and the balance must be restored. She has betrayed us.'

He took out his chisel. Duke was right.

He bent over Ciara and cut through her clothes. She awoke as he did, and he grabbed her chin to hold her head up sobbing as he pressed the blade down and she felt the cold kiss of steel as it broke flesh before the warmth of blood alarmed her. She could barely see through tears as she thrashed but Earl had pinned her down and was also crying as he carved a large seven unto her head.

"I am so sorry, Ciara." He repeated through tears.

Just then, the door was kicked open and Anita Heath ran into the room, gun drawn. She was the first to enter the apartment and had rushed into the bedroom. The other policemen were checking the other rooms. They had been on their way to Earl's house when the 911 call came in. Anita had sent some men over to his house while she went to Ciara's house.

"Police! Drop your weapon!" She shouted, pointing her gun at the man standing over Ciara. His back was to her, so he raised his hands slowly and turned to face her.

"Hello Detective." He said, a smirk on his face.

"Earl..." She called quietly. She had seen his picture but seeing him face to face was even more shocking. It was almost like he had not aged a day from when they were kids. But then he stood before her and all his memories went up in smoke. His eyes were cold and stern as though he was staring off into space and had the most sinister smile.

"It is good to see you, Detective." He said, his face looking sad.

"You killed our mother," Anita stated, her face and voice emotionless.

Earl paused at a revelation.

"Ann…Yes." He replied, equally devoid of emotion. "Mother had the mark and had to go."

"What mark? You sick bastard!" She exclaimed; her gun still trained on him. The number on each of his victim's faces began to make sense.

"I'm the sick bastard? Who leaves their helpless brother alone with an abusing drunk?" He asked matter-of-factly as if everything was her fault.

The look on his face infuriated Anita. Any trace of pity she had for him evaporated when he bent over to reach for his chisel. But she had to contain the situation. He was still bending over Ciara and Anita could not predict what he would do. She took deep breaths to control herself and contain her anger.

"Um, Earl. I know I did not do right, and I should have taken you and momma along with me when I left. I am sorry." Anita said, trying to look as sorry as she could when she was just angry.

"You are sorry now, eh?" He asked, a smirk on his face. He had dropped the chisel when he raised his hands.

"Yes, I am. We can make this right, and I can be a better sister. Only just…don't do anything bad again. Please. I know it is all my fault." Anita pleaded tears in her eyes, and she could see him softening.

Earl looked at his sister and began to sob.

"I am sorry. I am so sorry." He said, covering his face with his hands.

'You weak bastard. You wimp. I knew you could not do it!' Duke's raspy voice said.

"Shut up, Duke. It's over, and I'm done with your bullshit!" Earl shouted at no one.

A good look at him told Anita that he was struggling with some demons he imagined were real. She approached him gently, walking with her left arm in front of her and her gun in the other hand. Ciara, who had regained her consciousness and was reeling from a horrible headache. She was in pain and seeing Earl, and she realized what he had done. Ciara could never forgive him. She stole the opportunity seeing Earl was distracted; she picked the chisel he had dropped and stabbed it hard in the stomach without a second thought.

"AARRGGGGHHH! You bitch! I am going to kill you." Duke exclaimed, his eyes blazing.

No, this was not Earl at all, Anita concluded. This was a demon. He pulled the chisel out from his stomach, where Ciara had stabbed him and lifted it above his head. He was snarling and spittle blood out of his mouth in a rage. He brought it down to stab Ciara. Just as Anita opened fire, firing twice in his direction. One shot hit Earl on the left arm and another in the side of his neck. He froze, the chisel fell from his lose grip and his body fell heavily on the bed, on top of Ciara, who began to scream. Anita quickly approached the bed, pushed Earl's lifeless body off her, and helped her to her feet.

Anita placed Ciara's arm across her shoulder and led her out of the bedroom and out of the apartment to the ambulance, where paramedics attended to her. Anita went back into the apartment and walked toward the bedroom. Pete was just walking out of the room when she stepped back into the apartment.

"Where is he?" She asked Pete, and he was already shaking his head.

"He's gone. All that's left is the number seven written in blood on the floor."

EPILOGUE

Ciara sat on her bed having woken up from a nightmare. It was one of those nights. It had been a year, but she still had this nightmare. Thankfully, it was morning. She was not sure she would be able to bear it if the night were any longer. She rubbed her face and felt the mark on her forehead. She hated looking in the mirror. She hated the permanent reminder of her ordeal with that mad man. She had taken to wearing bangs or beanies to avoid people's pitying stares. It was not easy, but she was glad to be alive.

Months of therapy had not helped, and she was beginning to despair of it. The police had never found Earl's body which did not make her feel better at all. She had thought about leaving Crest Hill but ultimately decided against it, thinking Earl had ultimately won whether he was dead or alive if she left. She had mourned Vinny and thankfully, Tonya had remained by her to comfort her. She sighed and got up from the bed. She went into her bathroom to wash her face. She slept with all the lights these days and could not manage a dark room.

She toweled her face dry and walked into the living room. She lived in constant fear that he would show up at her doorstep at any time since they had not found his body. She dressed for the day and got ready to go out. There was a knock on her door. Tonya was early today, she thought. Tonya always came to her house so that they could walk to work together.

She opened the door, but it wasn't Tonya at the door.

His face was overgrown with his beard, and he had colored his dark hair light, but she would recognize those brown eyes anywhere.

"Hi, Ciara." He said as he pushed the door open. ***"WE MISSED YOU"***

She fell down and he dragged her into the room just like he had that day.

Her nightmare had just come back to life.